Praise for Meike Ziervogel

'Meike Ziervogel is becoming one of the most interesting
figures in the contemporary British and European
world, not just because she is a publisher of imagination
and daring, but a writer of grace, forensic precision,
and power. Rarely has someone given so much from
sheer enthusiasm, and talent, and been so worth
watching.' NICHOLAS LEZARD, *Guardian* critic

Praise for *Magda*

'This was by far the most intense, impressive and
unexpected book on the shortlist. It's the one that
provoked the strongest emotional and intellectual reaction
and more simply seemed to me to be the best written.'
SAM JORDISON, *Guardian*, Not the Booker Prize

'Challenging, clever, and fascinating as an insight
into how generations of Germans are summoning
the courage to address the horror of the last
century.' AMANDA CRAIG, *Independent*

'Ziervogel is the brave woman who set up Peirene
Press five years ago . . . Her own debut novel displays
similar nerve . . . This is an ambitious and queasily
unsettling novel.' DAVID MILLS, *Sunday Times*

'The deftly arranged sequence of scenes gradually reveals the fears and needs of each protagonist and their relationships with each other, outlined with a careful, thoughtful style that creates an unusual atmosphere of charged bleakness. Strange, but oddly impressive.' HARRY RITCHIE, *Daily Mail*

'Ziervogel's prose is generally superb, with true flair and an originality that is rare when confronting such an everyday subject.' ROISIN O'CONNOR, *Independent on Sunday*

'Stark and acutely observed realism . . . The result is visceral, bleak and moving.' CLAIRE HAZELTON, *Guardian*

'At a striking pace, the narrative switches between the perspectives of different characters, and the sense of emotional disconnect between them becomes ever more visceral and claustrophobic.' ANNA SAVVA, *The Lady*

MEIKE ZIERVOGEL grew up in Germany and came to London in 1986 to study Arabic. In 2008 she founded Peirene Press, an award-winning, London-based, independent publishing house. *Kauthar* is Meike's third novel. Find out more about Meike at www.meikeziervogel.com

By the same author

Magda
Clara's Daughter

KAUTHAR

Meike Ziervogel

CROMER

PUBLISHED BY SALT
12 Norwich Road, Cromer, Norfolk NR27 0AX United Kingdom

Printed in Great Britain by Clays Ltd, St Ives plc

Typeset in Sabon 10/13

This book is a work of fiction. Names, characters, businesses, organizations,
places and events are either the product of the author's imagination or used
fictitiously. Any resemblance to actual persons, living or dead, events or
locales is entirely coincidental.

ISBN 978 1 78463 029 4 paperback

1 3 5 7 9 8 6 4 2

KAUTHAR

'It's the English woman.'

Razor-sharp, the voice penetrates my ear. Have they found my passport? Unveiled my face? Ripped off my clothes? I see dim outlines of bodies moving. Electric cables flutter in the wind, black smoke glides past. I hear screams. Why are they screaming? Yellow and red flames surround me. Shards of metal touch my fingers.

'Jeez!'

The same voice. Johnson?

Why am I still here? Why are they still here? I wanted to take them with me. To show them the way. The only way. They can't find it on their own. Because they are blind. They believe they can hide their blindness. From You. From me. Hide it beneath bullet-proof helmets. Behind dark sunglasses which reflect the country where once Your Garden of Eden flourished and grew. They destroyed it with their bombs and their unbelief; placed their tanks and their barriers in the way. But to no avail. Your garden will grow again and spread across the world. And the infidels will be punished. I have put myself to the test. All power is with You. You are the Creator of everything that is created out of nothing. You hold life and death in Your hands. God, I am ready. Lead me into Your mercy, into Your divine Paradise.

I

Hubb – Love

'K<small>AUTHAR</small>.'

I glance quickly to my left. A tall man is rising from the park bench. I'd already caught sight of him out of the corner of my eye as I left the building. It is a mild summer's evening in Jumaada al-awwal 1421. The square is deserted. Only this man and me. The other students of the Arabic evening class left more than half an hour ago. I stayed behind in the language lab. I now lower my gaze, forcing myself to keep a steady pace. I don't want to give the impression of being frightened. I'm heading towards the metal gates that separate the university from Malet Street. I am wearing an ankle-length cotton skirt and a dark-blue summer blazer over a long-sleeved blouse. My feet in flat sandals are covered by socks despite the warm weather. My hair, neck and shoulders are concealed by a dark-grey hijab. I am a *muhajabah* and he, an Arab judging by his complexion, ought to know that he shouldn't shout after me in public. I have never seen this man before. Perhaps he is confusing me with someone else. Other women are called Kauthar too. Or maybe I misheard.

'Please wait.'

He has raised his voice so I can still hear him. He hasn't moved.

'I would like to propose to you.'

There is a brief pause. I take another step.

'I would like to marry you.'

On the road a black cab drives past. I put my left foot forward. Then I stop. But I don't turn around. Lydia would have laughed out loud now. No man with serious intentions chats up a woman on the street in the middle of London. No sane man asks a woman he has never met before to marry him. This man must be backward in some way. He has picked up the phrase, knows roughly in which context to use it, but has no idea of its emotional connotations. Basically, a little boy who is playing his games – cowboys and Indians, for example. And he chooses a bride and takes her into his tent.

≈

'Willy, willy. Dick.' *Ratatata*. 'Willy, willy. Dick.' *Ratatata*. 'Willy, willy. Dick.' *Ratatata*.

Rushing wind fills Lydia's ears. She can barely understand what Marcus is yelling. But she can hear him calling out these names and she can hear the rattling of the beer mats he has fastened to the spokes of his wheels. He is circling the playground on his bicycle. Lydia is hanging head-down from the highest monkey bar, swinging back and forth. Marcus's blonde hair appears and disappears above the wooden fence to the rhythm of her movement.

'Willy, willy. Dick.' *Ratatata*. 'Willy, willy. Dick.' *Ratatata*. 'Willy, willy. Dick.' *Ratatata*.

Lydia doesn't like Marcus. His constant chatter about willies gives her the creeps. And when they play spin the bottle with the others in the trees behind the church he always insists on tongue-kissing. At school he is one of the cool boys – denim jacket, jeans, hangs out with the likes of Charlie – and would never be seen anywhere near Lydia and Kathy. But in the holidays he's often alone.

'Then show us your willy. Come on,' shouts Kathy.

She is sitting sideways on top of the middle monkey bar, coy, one leg bent, one straight. Kathy is Lydia's best friend. She is already twelve and last year she had a boyfriend from the fourth form.

'Do you think I'd show him to just any girl?' Marcus calls back.

'I'll tell you what I think.' Kathy's straight leg is kicking the air playfully. 'I think—' she pauses for dramatic effect – 'you have a teeny-weeny one.'

'You must be joking. I've got the biggest dick ever. You've never seen anything like it.'

'Show us. Come on. You're a coward. You won't even get

off your bike. Why don't you stop, climb up that tower and show us what you've got?'

A high wooden fence encloses the rectangular playground and in each corner there is a tower, like in a fort.

'Show him to your ugly face? The very thought makes me feel sick!' He pretends to throw up, then continues his monotonous song.

'Willy, willy. Dick.' *Ratatata*. 'Willy, willy. Dick.' *Ratatata*. 'Willy, willy. Dick.' *Ratatata*. Like the howling of a lonely wild beast.

Lydia is happy that she doesn't need to participate in this exchange. She is watching the ends of her two pigtails floating above the sandy ground. They are not flying through the air yet because she is still swinging with care. Sometimes she would love to cut her hair as short as Nadia Comăneci's. Nadia's hair is not really short, but shorter than Lydia's. Her mother says short hair only suits dark-haired girls. Dark-haired girls always have very thick hair. Lydia's hair is ash blonde and thin.

If she had hair like Nadia Comăneci she might be good at gymnastics. But Lydia is not good. She is scared of the bar, the vault, the beam. She is scared of stumbling, falling off, breaking a bone, knocking out a tooth. She doesn't want to hit her head so that it bleeds. Most girls in her year can do the back hip circle on the bar. Kathy can. Lydia can't. She can only hang head-down. Of course she would love to be able to do the hip circle, but she will never learn how to because she is scared. And really, to be scared of gymnastics is silly. Especially since

6

her father used to be a leading gymnast and almost became a member of the 1960 Olympic team in Rome, and then again in 1964 in Tokyo. However, that was long before Lydia was born. And now he loves running, and runs every day for an hour or two when he is at home, with a stopwatch in his hand. Lydia, meanwhile, tries to cheat her way through the sports lessons. She puts on a stoical face, pretending it doesn't matter that everyone is better than her, while encouraging her class-mates to have their go ahead of her in the hope that the school bell will ring before her turn comes around.

~

This man, however, is not backward, and he doesn't play games, especially not in relation to something as sacred as a marriage proposal. He knows that marriage is a sacrament. He's a Muslim. He obeys Allah's will. And Kauthar doesn't play such games either. Now Lydia, yes, she would have want-ed to play. She would have laughed, or carried on walking with a smile. She might have hoped that the man would follow her; not chase her, but attempt to get her attention. Would she have stopped? She couldn't have, because she would have run the risk of becoming a laughing stock. Did you honestly think I wanted to marry you – just like that? Who do you think you are? A film star? A supermodel? And if she had gone with him – to the pub, of course, to have a drink and lose her inhibi-tions – and they'd ended up in bed together, the next morning he would have said, What, marry you! Which century are you living in? We had a good fuck, that's all.

So Lydia would have kept on walking, would have gone home, into the lonely silence. And in order to bear it she would have drunk one or two or three glasses of wine. Then, in the following days, she'd have gone into work, taking the bus, the Tube, while all the time fantasizing, hoping, that she would see the man again; that he would be looking for her, waiting for her, because he wanted to meet her again just as much as she wanted to meet him. And while she walked down the road, she'd look out for him. Sometimes she'd be convinced that he was coming towards her, only to be disappointed. Or in the library, when someone came in, she'd be sure she could feel their gaze on her back. She would not turn around immediately, pretending not to have noticed his presence. Eventually of course she would look over her shoulder, only to find herself staring into a void or at someone she had never seen before. Her heart would be in a permanent state of erratic expectation, her body wired. But nothing would happen. And she'd regret not having stopped.

That's how it would have been with Lydia.

But she is not Lydia.

I am not Lydia. I am no longer Lydia. I have never been Lydia. I should never have been Lydia.

Lydia died at the age of eleven, the summer after Nadia Comăneci won the gold medal in Montreal.

~

The girl is now swinging more vigorously. Her pigtails are flying through the air. Perhaps it's the rushing wind in her ears that excludes everything else, even the fear. Anyway, suddenly she knows that no one and nothing will disturb her practice, that finally she has all the time in the world and one day, perhaps even in the next sports lesson, she will be able to swing and straddle and perform a front flyaway. And she will finish her routine like Nadia Comăneci; pelvis pushed forward, a beautiful curve in her back, both feet firmly rooted to the ground, legs slightly apart, arms stretched up high, head thrown back, mouth laughing. The audience applauds. She has accomplished the impossible. It's amazing. Lydia feels the cold metal of the monkey bar in the hollows behind her knees. She becomes even more courageous, swings further back. She watches her fingertips skimming the hard, sandy ground before they once more lift up towards the sky. Her pigtails have disappeared. Instead she now sports a beautiful short haircut and her hair blows softly in the wind, gently brushing her cheeks. She sees Kathy's blue jacket, hears her giggles. Once again she spots Marcus's blonde hair gliding above the fence. Individual images, disjointed, fading into the distance with each swing. Lydia is now the brave, poised gymnast. The newcomer. The rising star. No one has paid much attention to her up to this moment. She has been inconspicuous. Overlooked. Underrated. But suddenly, literally overnight, she has turned the corner. All the hard practice and training and discipline has been worth it. Her progress is unbelievable. But will she succeed? Will she be courageous enough to try a full twisting flyaway? No. That's impossible. Only yesterday she was a mere schoolgirl. And today the eyes of the country, of the whole world, are upon her. One more push. Her body flies backwards. She is still feeling the cold metal bar behind her knees. Her back is straight, arms extended above her head. Her body is at the same level as the bar. She has never swung that high. For a moment she is in limbo. No gravity is pulling her. She is floating. Then her heart begins to race. She knows the moment has come. It's now or never. When she swings forward she will jump and land, legs slightly apart, with both feet firmly on the ground. Her head tipped back, she will throw her arms up into the air, her back beautifully curved. And then a smile, a happy, tired smile, will appear on her lips. She sees it all in her mind's eye. Her body already carries the memory of the image inside her, a future that has already happened, a future that has been programmed to happen.

The forward swing has begun.

'Willy, willy. Dick.' *Ratatata*. 'Willy, willy. Dick.' *Ratatata*.

The hollows behind her knees peel away from the bar. Flip, tuck, pike, hecht, salto, swing, straddle. Beautiful words that she knows from the television. They sound rounded and full; their mere utterance gives the illusion that the exercise has been performed faultlessly. A perfect 10 without doubt. The crowd is ecstatic. Will Lydia McArthur be the first ever to achieve 10.1? The nation's hopes are pinned on her. She is airborne.

But.

Her legs aren't straight. They should be straight, not tucked. She won't achieve the 10.1. For an incomprehensible, fleeting moment Lydia knows that she has failed.

And she hits the ground. Her knees slam on to the hard floor. A jolt travels through her body. Then it moves no more. For a split second she struggles to comprehend. Her mind can't process quickly enough what has happened. Without understanding, in total ignorance, she is kneeling on the floor. Waiting. A moment of mercy and grace. Then her brain begins to receive and decipher the signals. She can't breathe! Panic grips her. She bends forward, presses her hands against her chest. Her mouth is open, but no air enters her lungs.

She hears the blood rushing in her ears and Marcus is still circling the playground. 'Willy, willy. Dick.' *Ratatata*. And Kathy is still shouting: 'Show us your willy, show us your willy. Coward. Show-off. Loser.'

And then suddenly.

Silence.

And Lydia knows she will die.

A vast, peaceful feeling has now taken possession of her. It fills her, is all around her. A white, clean blanket has been spread over her. The panic has gone. Kathy and Marcus have gone. The playground, the monkey bar, Nadia Comăneci – all gone. Nothing matters any longer. There is only that beautiful, wonderful, all-encompassing calm. Around her, inside her, she is part of it, at one with it. Her hands are resting in her lap, she is surrendering to the inevitable. There is no more running, no more fighting, no more longing. That belongs to a world in which she is no longer present.

And in this calm, her life plays out in front of her eyes one last time. A single image and yet innumerable tiny ones. The big picture is static, framed as if it hangs in a museum where it has always hung and always will. The little ones are moving, rolling past, unfolding in front of her, flickering. This is Lydia's life: every event, every person, every place, every thought, every dream she has ever experienced, spoken to, seen, thought, dreamed. She is allowed to glance at everything one last time, as an observer. She is allowed to experience it all one more time, not sequentially, as a succession of finite moments, but as a single endless moment. Her life, her being, is being revealed to her, in eternity, for eternity. And she knows, afterwards, that she will have to go. The last deed that remains to be done. And it is an unbounded, calm, immeasurably light feeling.

～

Only He knows what comes after. I will leave my body behind. Soon. Very soon. I am lying in the middle of a desert. Nothing but sand all around me. Dry, yellow sand. There is nothing I can hold on to, no beginning, no middle, no end. What am I doing in this desert? How did I get here? I don't know, but I have to get out. Because of my love for Him. I would like to whisper, I love You. So that He might lift me up, away from here, into the Other. Into His reality. But my lips don't move. Can't move. My body can't perform this movement any longer. Can't perform any movement. Because it is torn apart. To what extent, I do not know. I can't see anything either. I can't tell if my eyes are open or closed. I think they are closed, but maybe it only seems that way to me and the outside world sees them as open. It doesn't matter. No one can reach me any more. In a moment I will be dead to these people. My body is dying and my soul has to be freed. This is how it is written. It can't be otherwise.

~

Air rushes into Lydia's lungs. She starts breathing again. And the picture, her life, shatters. Just fragments. She bends forward, presses her fist into her stomach, her forehead touches the ground. She coughs. Her face is bright red. Marcus is still circling the playground. Kathy is still sitting on the middle monkey bar.

'Are you OK? Do you want me to hit you on the back?' Kathy asks.

Lydia shakes her head, waving her hand in the air. Everything is fine. She feels silly, even though neither Marcus nor Kathy have realized what really happened. Marcus is still talking about his willy; Kathy is still giggling and teasing.

And Lydia bends forward again.

~

And my forehead touches the floor and I press my hands flat under my shoulders. I tuck my toes in and pray: *Subhana rabbiyal a'la. Subhana rabbiyal a'la. Subhana rabbiyal a'la.* Three times. Glory to my Lord, the Highest. Glory to my Lord, the Highest. Glory to my Lord, the Highest. And the breath that I take in with these words fills my chest, I feel my heart as light as a feather and I feel the air that travels from my chest into my stomach and to my spine. The path from the playground to here was long: from the playground, where for the first time I fell into the most God-fearing position, where I prostrated myself in front of God without knowing what I was doing. My movements came from my deepest unconscious, born out of my soul's desire to prostrate itself in front of the Creator. My childlike soul apprehended then what my head would understand only years later. In the playground, in front of the monkey bars on my knees, I met the Creator Himself, came closer to Him than ever again since. The calm that I perceived then, the quietness that surrounded me, is not from this world, has nothing to do with this life. Peace was upon me. A peace which can stem only from devotion to God. He is all-knowing and wise. He knows His creatures. But we no longer know Him. If only I had understood then what had happened to me: that I had recognized God and fallen to my knees in front of Him. He didn't take me in. You didn't take me in. Why not? Was it because I was a child who didn't yet turn to You knowingly?

And I sit up straight. *Allahu akbar*. For a moment I remain on my knees, only to prostrate myself once more in front of You, *Allahu akbar*. No, I am not throwing myself down. Instead I slide down slowly, I bend my head, I lower my body; my hands are touching the ground, fingers slightly spread. An elegant, gracious movement. A dance performance. A gymnast's routine. Out of the corner of my eye I see the women to my right and left. Eight or ten women. We are all part of the same movement. I see Rabia's hand next to mine, her pale fingers with the beautifully manicured nails, unvarnished. How often have I seen this hand touch the ground next to mine, felt her body bend in submission next to mine? How often have I secretly admired her flawless movements in honour and praise of the Almighty, the Most Beautiful?

~

At the beginning, when I ask Rabia to show me how to pray, I just watch. Eventually I decide to stand beside her. I haven't yet learned the words. I raise my hands when she lifts hers up to her ears, palms facing forward. Then I lower my arms to the sides of my thighs, following Rabia's example, standing upright, waiting while she begins quietly to praise Allah. Her lips are moving, but no sound escapes as she asks Him to protect her from the devil, reciting the first Sura of the Quran. I have only a vague idea of the words of the Muslim prayer, but I want to imitate the movement. I want to see what it feels like.

And in unison with my friend Rabia I bend my upper body forward and place my hands on my knees. Again I am waiting, but I have already learned that we won't stay in this position for long. *Ruku'* is followed by *qiyam* – to stand up straight. And then we lower ourselves on to our knees in order to bow down in *sujud* – the prostrate position. *Ruku'*, *qiyam*, *sujud*. These are my first words in Arabic. They are magic words, describing the skills required to perform a beautiful routine of submission, prayer and praise.

My routine, which I have worked on for many years, has now been perfected.

~

The day Rafiq approaches me, I am Kauthar. I have been Kauthar for a long time, all the time, returned home to where I belong, and my rules are the rules of Allah, and I follow His laws and His laws are lucid. If a Muslim man approaches a Muslim woman with a view to marrying her, his intentions must be honest. Because God doesn't like hypocrites.

'I am sorry to approach you like this. I've been waiting for you. I'm Rafiq Ismail.'

He walks towards me and stops about three steps in front of me.

'How do you know my name?'

A strong nose, full lips, well-defined eyebrows and, beneath them, dark eyes with long lashes. He is clean-shaven, a few grey hairs at the temples, tiny wrinkles at the corners of his mouth. He is wearing a light-blue casual shirt, the top two buttons open, and a pair of beige trousers. A man, not a boy.

'The first time I saw you was in the library where I was looking for some books.'

His English is flawless, educated. He must have gone to a good school. No accent. Only a slight off-beat in the melody betrays the fact that English is not his first language. He looks straight at me. He is used to looking women in the eye.

'Then I saw you again at the Islamic Centre, on the eve of Sayyida Fatimah's *mawlid*.'

So he is a Shiite.

'And a month ago I spotted you for the third time. Here. I came to meet my friend Mr Alim.'

Mr Alim is my teacher. A lovely man from Syria, probably in his late fifties, with a very nice wife who must be as wide as she is high. I like Mr Alim very much, even though he doesn't think highly of his own religion, Islam. But he is clever and knows as much about Western literature as he knows about Arabic books, and he is a gifted language teacher.

'When I saw you for the third time, I knew this was a sign from Allah. I asked Alim about you. He told me of your natural linguistic skills and how easily you picked up even a complicated language such as Arabic. He told me about your inquisitive mind and your devotion to Allah. But he couldn't tell me if you are married. He thinks you are not, because no man ever accompanies you here or picks you up. Mr Alim knows that for a while now I've been looking for a wife. He knows I am choosy and he knows me well. He promised me that he would ask his wife to find out more about you.'

And I remember bumping into Mrs Alim two weeks ago.

At the end of the lesson Mr Alim asks me to stay behind. He hands me another text to translate for practice at home. As I am heading out of the classroom, I nearly collide with Mrs Alim in the doorway. Mr Alim briefly introduces us. I leave them and walk along the silent, dark corridor. Suddenly I hear Mrs Alim calling after me. She hurries to catch up. Her husband still has work to do, she doesn't have time to wait for him. Would I mind accompanying her to the bus stop? She doesn't like walking on her own in the evening. Of course I agree. She puts her arm in mine. We are walking very slowly. She's got something wrong with her foot, she explains, and because she rushed to catch me up it's hurting again. We take the lift down, then we are heading towards Russell Square to the bus stop. She complains a bit about her foot, then she grumbles a bit about Mr Alim and says that he takes his teaching more seriously than his marriage. She laughs and asks if my husband displays similar tendencies. I shake my head.

'I hope you don't misunderstand me,' she continues. 'Mr Alim and I love and honour each other very much. We got married when I was fifteen and he seventeen.'

'*Mash'Allah*. Allah willed it. *Mash'Allah, ya tant*,' I call out to express my true admiration, but also because I know she is expecting me to say it.

'Does your husband love you?'

She limps along beside me, smiling. In our Western culture this small question, asked by the by, would most likely be interpreted as intrusive if not downright rude. Whether my husband loves me or not is a private matter. In the Islamic culture, however, such a question is fuelled by sincere sympathy, maternal concern, an older woman cares for a younger woman and wants to make sure that she is OK.

I answer truthfully, 'Unfortunately I am not married.'

'*Insh'Allah*, soon, God willing,' she replies, squeezing my arm gently. 'It is not good for a beautiful young woman to be alone.' The bus approaches. She takes my face between her hands, presses a wet kiss on my right cheek and then my left, and reassures me once more, '*Insh'Allah*, God willing, you will find a husband very soon.'

≈

Two weeks ago I didn't think much about her last words. I took them as a polite phrase, as small talk, something she felt obliged to say but that was beyond her realm of influence. Now I smile as I remember this little round woman limping along next to me. I wouldn't have guessed that she had such a crafty side to her.

I say it out loud: 'She didn't look as crafty as that at all. I am impressed.'

Even while I am still speaking I see the tension disappearing from Rafiq's face and a broad smile appearing on his lips.

'Well, she is an Arab woman.'

For a moment we fall silent. I have averted my eyes once again and my thoughts return to Lydia, and how much Lydia would have loved to meet such a man. A man who had noticed her long before she saw him. She had grown in importance, been given a place in his life, before she even knew of his exist- ence. Like a father who has a vague idea of his daughter's life before she is born, who holds her in his arms as a baby, his eyes resting upon her, this beautiful female creature that he has fathered, the most beautiful female creature he has ever seen. And her eyes are still closed, but when she opens them she will see him, he who has already known about her for months. He who has already admired her all her life, in whose arms she will find protection, who will show her the world. All her life long Lydia has waited for such a man.

~

And she feels his soft, full lips and thinks, he is forty-five, six foot tall, and weighs at least 16 stone, a mature man, a successful banker, and I am twenty-two, he could be my father. It is July – the notorious month of affairs in Paris, when men send their wives and children to the south of France on holiday, to the seaside or the countryside, in order to clear the way for a blonde, blue-eyed English tourist. And Claude is leaning across the little round table and the wicker chair creaks and he kisses Lydia. She hears the cars honking on the

Rue de Rivoli. She observes how the red liquid sloshes about in the wine glass under his weight on the table and makes a bet in her head whether drops will spill on to the green tabletop. Still, she allows him to kiss her and responds to his kiss, because she doesn't want to waste her time this week. They are three student teachers pretending to be into art and culture for a few days in Paris. Liz and Jane both have boyfriends, also student teachers, and Lydia has Pete, a handyman, a lovely bloke with a motorbike and huge hands, with whom she can only go to bed when she is totally drunk. But he adores her. She likes it that he adores her and is proud of her, and that he picks her up on his motorbike whenever she wants. And they speed down to London and back. Then they go to the pub and drink and afterwards retreat to the shed in the garden of the house where he lives with his mother. In the early hours of the morning Pete drives her back into Norwich, to the flat she shares with Liz and Jane. She takes a shower to wash off all the shame and disgust and then slides beneath the clean sheets, happy that she is finally alone. If only she had stayed at home that evening to revise and study, or gone netball training like Jane. But Lydia has never played netball. Or perhaps gone to the stables like Liz. But animals have always frightened Lydia, especially horses. Therefore maybe it's best with Pete. He is there for her whenever she calls him. He finishes his job at five on the dot, he is a good handyman, a nice man who is also looking after his mum, who had a stroke far too early in life. And his mum has a little house that he will inherit one day. Lydia imagines that they will sell it and buy an old farm near the coast. And Pete will do up the farm and convert the barn too as a study for her. And Lydia will be the head teacher at a nearby primary school, and they will have two happy children, and Lydia will be happy, and once or twice a month she will visit Liz and Jane in Norwich to go to the cinema. Many people are amazed that Pete and Lydia are so contented, because intellectually she is miles ahead of him. But they are contented because he adores her. And without her he doesn't know what to do, even now, after only two months of knowing her. He idolizes her and tells her that she could become a professor if she wanted to.

'What kind of professor?' Lydia asks.

'A professor,' he replies, slightly amazed by her question. Then he shrugs his shoulders. 'A professor is a professor and you are so clever.'

Finally she is lying in her bed, clean and pure, with only one wish: that the roller coaster in her head might stop and she might never drink again. Dear God, please. I promise never again. And she despises herself for sleeping with Pete. She imagines the old farmhouse near the coast and her study in the converted barn and how she will teach at the school and sleep with Pete every now and again, and how she will be happy because she has finally understood that this is what happiness means. Her stomach churns. Luckily she has already placed a bowl next to the bed. Afterwards she keeps very still. She feels lonely and guilty because Pete loves her but she does not love him. And she is disgusted by herself that she allows him to touch her, that she ever allowed a man to touch her. She would love to be a nun, clean and pure and innocent and in love with only Him. She opens her eyes and stares at the ceiling. She tries to concentrate on the small lampshade which is visible because of the glow from the street light. The lampshade doesn't remain fixed in one spot; it slips from her sight, spins and turns and dances around in circles there on the ceiling.

∽

But she doesn't want to become a teacher, doesn't want to live in a converted barn. She wants to escape the smallness, the narrowness. She wants to move. I want to move. Have I still got legs? Arms? I can't see any longer, neither the world out-side nor inside myself. I sit in front of a black hole, stare down into a deep shaft. I am sitting in the desert. I am on my knees. I bend forward to stare down into the deep black shaft in order to pray. Muhammad, peace be upon him, and all the other prophets before him – Abraham, Moses, Jesus – came from the desert. To each one of us He reveals signs, again and again, because He is all-merciful, all-patient, the father who knows about the blindness of His children. He is also the Wise One and so He knows that His children, especially the disobedient ones, will come to their senses with experience. Today, when clarity is upon me, I am grateful to Him. Infinitely grateful. And I fall to my knees in front of Him and I submit to Him, till my forehead touches the ground. For a moment I remain without thought, without words, without breath, so as to feel His breath penetrate deep inside me. And I am filled with the knowledge of His Love.

Alas, I can no longer perform this act of devotion. I am lying paralysed on a dusty road, unable to move. Has my body been ripped apart?

And I am back in the bed, and I still have arms and I still have legs, and my stomach is smooth and soft and closed, and I wish it would open up so that I could tear out all the ugly, disgusting, dirty stuff I put inside. I would like to die, so that everything can come to an end. And I would like to be clean and pure and innocent like a baby, a newborn, who has just come from Him and will return to Him.

~

Lydia leans back in her chair and crosses her legs. Her hem rides up. She is wearing a tight skirt that finishes just above the knee, typical for Parisian women. She bought it yesterday at Tati's and today she has put her hair up and tied a beautiful silk scarf around her neck, with the knot to one side. She is sure there is a Catherine Deneuve film in which she wears a scarf with her hair backcombed and up at the back. She takes the packet of Marlboro Lights between her thumb and index finger, places it upright and then lets it drop on to its narrow, long side. She says to Claude, 'Let's go.'

At the Gare du Nord she says goodbye to Liz and Jane, who are heading to Rome as planned.

'I will see you back in Norwich,' Lydia says.

In the small hotel just behind the Sacré-Cœur she changes to a single room. The following morning flowers are delivered – four lilac hydrangea heads – and black lace underwear that fits perfectly, even the bra.

At the end of the month, the month of Parisian affairs, Claude has to pack and catch up with his family in Provence. He says to Lydia, 'Please move to London, so that we can remain lovers for longer than this month. I am in London on business every two weeks.' He throws out his bait. He is a seasoned and skilled hunter. 'I have connections in television there and can get you a job.'

~

Her mother's voice starts to break: 'Listen to me, I only want the best for you. What are you doing? Your friends are finishing off their teaching training. Why not you? And why go to London? It's too far away. There's a lot of crime there. I will be so scared thinking about you, I won't be able to sleep at night.' Big tears are running down her cheeks.

Lydia puts an arm around her mother. 'Don't worry. You'll see, I'll become a famous TV presenter. I'll earn enough money to travel back and forth, no problem.' She sits down next to her mother and takes her hand and strokes it gently.

And to her father she says, 'Dad, will you be proud of me if I become a famous TV presenter?'

'Teaching is a better job for a woman. Your mother used to help in the classroom when you were small,' he replies, and presses the button on his stopwatch again.

He had pressed it to stop and now he presses it to continue, because it is important that he keeps his time. When he was stationed with the army in Germany he ran the same distance on similar terrain – boggy marsh and moor – in 53 minutes 7 seconds with ease and no strain. He now often finds himself in the region of 58 minutes. This is unacceptable. He needs to intensify his training. As long as he remains under 58. That's a good time and many of the young soldiers nowadays would struggle to come close. They lift weights, look the part, but he can still outrun them. Stamina! That's what's needed. Where is your stamina? And his right thumb presses down on the button, the watch starts ticking and Lydia knows the short interlude during which her father sees to his other duties, such as family, is over.

For a moment she hesitates, her glance wandering across the lake to the right. The water is violet and the sky above shines watery blue. She steps off the path and into the bog, shifts her weight on to one leg, presses her foot into the moss that is filled with water like a wet sponge. And her trainer is soaked within seconds. They have always lived near moors. Her father loves moors. It's good training terrain. As a child Lydia never trusted the spongy moss, thought maybe you could drown in it, even though her father assured her otherwise. Or perhaps corpses lay hidden in it and would grab her by the ankle with their white bony hands to pull her down towards them. When they were stationed near Bremen, her father used to run on the Teufelsmoor – the devil's moor. For Lydia the name was proof enough that the ghosts of dead people were living in its depths, or at least corpses had been dumped there once upon a time and might resurface. At school she learned that Teufelsmoor comes from the colloquial German Duvels-moor, and that *duvel* refers to barren land because nothing except peat and cotton grass grows there. But she still doesn't trust moors. Because names aren't just hollow signs without meaning.

She retrieves her foot from the mossy sponge to catch up with the former competitive gymnast who nearly made it in 1960 to Rome and in 1964 to Tokyo, the ex-army officer, her father.

In the back garden of their house, where he installed a pull-up bar, she is now watching him doing his daily fifty pull-ups. Then he smiles at her and changes his grip, turns the other way and swings back and forth. He lets go of the bar in a backwards movement, turns 180 degrees in mid-air and lands on both feet, knees and torso slightly bent. And as he is about to straighten up he takes both arms backwards, then brings them forward with a single smooth, powerful movement and uses that momentum to help him jump forward and grab the bar once more. Ten further pull-ups. Then bar release. 'That's enough for today,' he says with a happy smile on his face. He picks up the stopwatch he placed on a tree trunk and he presses the button once more, because next he will jog around the garden for four minutes to cool down.

It's now Lydia's turn to jump up at the bar: her hands grip it and she tries to pull herself up, her legs kicking the air as though she is swimming underwater, but the bar slips from her hands.

~

'I am happy to talk about marriage,' says Kauthar.

Rafiq smiles and replies, 'I am a Shiite and you are a Shiite. I know that I want to marry you and stay with you forever. You are the woman I have searched for all my life.'

We are still standing underneath the ash trees in the empty square. Since he called my name perhaps one or two minutes have passed, as measured by time elapsed on this earth. At a deeper level, though, time is measured differently and on this scale an eternity has gone by since we first met. But in fact it is only our bodies that have stood here. Our souls have already travelled together to the end of time and back. And now this very moment we have arrived here at this spot and it makes total sense that he has spoken these words. Only for an outsider would his sentences appear as if plucked out of thin air, illogical, without context – even silly. But not for him or for me. For neither Rafiq nor Kauthar.

'Still,' he continues, 'I can't blame you if at the moment you think, What does this man want? I don't know him. How does he dare to talk to me? That's why I want to propose a *zawaj muta*' – a temporary marriage. On your terms. So you have time to get to know me.' He closes his mouth. Looks at me.

I say, 'OK.'

I don't know how to continue. A temporary marriage on my terms – that means I can set the time limit, ask for a dowry and also decide if, during this time, we will have physical contact.

I smile and say, 'I don't know what else to say.'

He, too, smiles. No. He laughs. His hands are still buried in the pockets of his beige trousers. His shoulders are twitching, then his entire body starts to shake with laughter.

'I am so happy that you agree. I haven't slept for three nights.'

He holds me with his gaze and his torso leans slightly forward. I would love to touch him.

'*Mabruk! Mabruk!* Congratulations. Congratulations.'

Startled, we shoot apart, as if we have stood far too close for far too long. My heel hits a tree trunk. Mrs Alim waves at us.

'*Mabruk! Mabruk!*'

She stops a couple of metres away, panting. She catches her breath and lifts her right hand in front of her mouth and produces an ululation.

'I can tell from your faces – it's happy news.'

'*Ya tant*, what are you doing here?'

29

Rafiq throws a quick, worried glance in my direction. He looks like a little boy caught in the act of committing a misdemeanour. Later he admits he was horrified that in that very moment he might have lost everything, because Mrs Alim's appearance looked as if it was prearranged.

'I couldn't stay at home and not know what was happening between the two of you. Mr Alim never tells me anything. And in any case, he's probably still upstairs and hasn't got a clue. So I decided I had to find out for myself.'

Before I even have time to greet her, she rushes towards me and hugs me.

'*Mabruk. Mabruk.*' She pinches my cheeks. 'You are a beautiful couple. I will leave the two of you alone now.'

Swiftly she turns on her heel and waddles in the direction of the uni building. Despite the weight of her body, her short legs and the panting, she climbs the stairs to the entrance with surprising agility. She disappears behind the glass doors.

'I didn't know she'd come. Honestly,' Rafiq says in a concerned tone.

Now it is my turn to laugh. And I feel happy and warm and would love Mrs Alim to be my mother. I could then run after her and ask her what I'm supposed to do next, what terms I should request. I have never entered into a *zawaj muta'* before.

Rafiq pulls the right hand out of his pocket and hands me a business card.

'Here is my card. Please call me when you are ready. I will wait. *Ma'salama, ya* Kauthar. Goodbye, Kauthar.'

He turns and heads in the opposite direction. Without looking at the card, I put it into the pocket of my jacket and only take it out again once I am sitting on the Tube. Rafiq Ismail, Anaesthetist. Then his home address in Tufnell Park – one Tube stop away from me.

≈

At home I search in my books to find out what to do and pray to Allah for instruction.

I remain on my knees, waiting in silence.

≈

And Claude throws his head back and is laughing with his mouth open, his blazer open, and his big belly shaking. He is laughing at Lydia after he has asked about her first childhood memory. So she told him about the clouds. How she would lie in her bed and stare out of the window for hours and choose the biggest, most luxuriant cloud. She would jump on it and travel far away. And when the cloud began to dissolve, she'd jump on to the next one. But sometimes she'd stay where she was because she had managed to attach herself to another cloud and bolster the one she was sitting on. For days Lydia would wonder if it were possible to live on a cloud. She wasn't concerned about building a house, finding something to eat – all these mundane concerns wouldn't matter if you lived on a cloud. Rather, she was wondering if she could float with and on the cloud, lie down on it, sleep there peacefully. If the cloud would hold her, never letting her go, so that she needn't fear it might dissolve beneath her. On the other hand, she was also looking for a cloud that she could leave if she wanted to, a cloud that wouldn't get upset if she decided to change. That was important to the girl. She didn't want clouds to be angry with her and dissolve in rage.

Claude is snorting with laughter. 'This is your first childhood memory?'

They are sitting in a chic London restaurant. Wood-panelled walls with black and white photographs of famous people who have dined here over the years. The photos are marked by signatures and thank-you notes. The waiters wear uniforms and from the street it is not possible to look inside the restaurant. Lydia will come here many more Thursday evenings.

'*C'est mignon.*' He finally shuts his mouth and leans forward across the table and strokes Lydia's cheek. 'You are sweet. And beautiful.' His hand moves underneath her chin. The smile disappears from his lips. '*Et je t'aime.*'

She feels her chin lying in his hand. For a moment she is confused. She didn't expect the last sentence. Even though Claude called her that afternoon at work. And at first she didn't understand he was calling from London. He wasn't supposed to be here until next week.

'I couldn't wait any longer. When can I see you?'

'Are you in London?'

'Give me your address and I will pick you up tonight at nine.'

Claude doesn't reply to questions. He is arrogant and she doesn't need to say yes. Even though he has now installed her here. Lydia thinks, *Il m'a installée*. For days, these words have been in her head. She's not working in a TV studio. It didn't work out, Claude said. Instead he found her a job as an assistant in an estate agency, where she makes a lot of coffee and sorts through papers. She won't stay there long, she thinks to herself. And she hasn't told her parents that she isn't working in TV – yet.

And she says yes to Claude, because she feels special and loved and honoured that he is already visiting her, that he couldn't wait.

'The fact that you are now living in London will make it all so much easier for us,' he says.

'You don't know if I want to continue with this affair. Now that I am here in London I might dump you,' she replies.

He looks at her silently.

'You want this affair. I know.'

'How do you know?'

'Because you have nothing to lose.'

'And you? Why do you want this affair?'

'Because it could lose me everything.'

So that's it. A game, where she has nothing to lose and can only win. At least, posh restaurants and nice hotels. She doesn't love him, and is convinced that she won't ever love him either. He has kids and a wife whom he won't leave. His family back in Paris serves as a limit, a barrier for her feelings, beyond which she can't, and doesn't want to, venture. She needs these limits, so that her feelings are kept in check, so that she doesn't imagine that he is the love of her life; the man with whom she will share the rest of her life, who will save her, like a knight on a white horse, who will recognize her for the person she is and through whom she will fulfil her real potential. Lydia accepts the *Je t'aime* as a clever move by him in the game, their game, Claude and Lydia's affair game. And within the logic of the game his words are sincere. He isn't lying. And she tells him about her cloud and he laughs, laughs at her, and she thinks, You are fat and arrogant and could be my father. And he says, I love you, and he kisses her across the table. For a moment she keeps her eyes open and sees his closing, feels his hand behind her ear, on her cheek. And behind him she sees the black and white celebrities and imagines, as she always imagined when she was a small girl, that proper kissing means turning the head from left to right and then from right to left. He gently bites her lower lip and she closes her eyes and senses his soft, full lips and his tongue in her mouth, and thinks, This is a game and I have nothing to lose.

~

I call Rafiq the next day and leave a message on his answer machine. I would like to enter a *zawaj muta'* for one month

34

and should there be any physical advances, they will come from me. The dowry is up to him. But as soon as I put down the receiver I am overcome by doubts. Was I too formal, too business-like? As I am sitting on the Tube on my way to work I try to calm myself. I try to convince myself that the manner in which I spoke was God's intention. All of this is out of my control. This is not my path but the one God has chosen for me. I have to follow it, wherever it may lead. With or without Rafiq. My egotistical self wants this man as my husband because I desire him. He brought Rafiq to me after I had searched for months for a husband and had asked my sisters, who introduced me to their brothers and relatives.

~

'I am pregnant,' Lydia says to Claude.

Two days ago, when the pink line appeared in the little plastic window of the pregnancy test, she was not surprised. It was an intended accident. She knows what she is doing. She worked at the estate agency for a year and then she found a job at the London Library. And every second Thursday Claude comes to London and they go out for a meal and afterwards to his hotel. When she is with Claude she wants to be his wife and she is convinced that for the last two and a half years she's just been waiting for the moment to become his wife. However, when she's back in her bedsit, she knows that she has to finish this affair, end this game, because the outcome will no longer be in her favour. She is losing. And so she plays her trump card. She falls pregnant. It's an accident. She didn't plan it. But a tiny door in the back of her mind stood open for this final move. She knows Claude will not leave his wife, he won't marry her. But now she will be his mistress with a child. His secret child. Only he and she will know about it. And of course the people she knows in London. But they won't know who the father is. And his wife will not know about the child either, as she doesn't even know about Lydia's existence. Lydia, however, knows everything about the other woman. Claude talks about her, complains about her, is bored with her. But he feels duty-bound to stay with her. He comes to Lydia because he wants to. She is his secret life. And now they will share a secret. Lydia will give birth to their child and the quest for a purpose in her life will thus become redundant.

And she tells Claude that she is pregnant. She is lying on top of him, her cheek is resting on his naked chest, her legs are open wide above his limp penis. It is Friday morning, five to seven. She can see the time on his watch on the bedside table. She wanted to tell him last night, but then she didn't. And now, even before she has finished pronouncing these three little words, she realizes it was the wrong moment.

'Who by?' he asks. Sleepily.

She watches the big hand as it moves on to the thin line before the number eleven. Claude loves traditional watches. She is still waiting for his chest to be lifted by laughter, although she already knows that this won't happen.

'Who by?' she eventually echoes his question.

'Yes, who by?'

He pushes her off his belly and sits up, swinging his feet over the edge of the bed. Lydia sees his back and a thin red line, which she must have drawn with her fingernail last night.

'By you. There is no one else.'

Her reply meets his back, then his bum as he stands up. She is looking at the watch once again. The big hand has moved on to three minutes to seven. Two more thin lines, then one final jump on to the big fat line and it will be seven o'clock. And she already knows that her life will be totally different at seven o'clock. She observers how Claude's fingers close around his watch.

'I thought you are taking the pill,' he says.

She can see his left wrist from the side. His right hand closes the locking mechanism. It shuts with a click.

'It was an accident,' she replies, as Claude walks into the bathroom. The door shuts.

For a moment she lies still, then she gets up, dresses, in no hurry but without pausing in her stride. The air around her feels thick and is holding her upright. She takes her bag and leaves before Claude reappears from the bathroom. She wishes she would be angry with him. Kick against the closed bathroom door, crash her fists into it, throw her body against it until he opens up. And then scream at him, hurl herself at his huge fat body, tear his hair out, kick him between the legs until he starts reacting, defending himself, hitting her. Or until he squirms on the floor

KAUTHAR

like a worm, and she will continue to boot him, right into his writhing, screaming body. His body, her body, it doesn't matter who is beating and who is getting beaten – as long as her anger abides. She sees the images in her mind's eye as she walks down the stairs: slowly, a step comes into view, then her foot, then the next step, then her other foot. An invisible glass bell jar ensures that she does not fall apart, is holding her together, in one piece, protects her and protects the world from her. No one can touch her and she can't touch anyone.

~

Claude calls. Lydia hears him say, 'We have to talk. I never thought you wanted a child from me. I always thought one day you would find someone younger who you would marry.'

She says, 'You hoped that you'd be rid of me.'

He says, 'I didn't hope for it, but I expected it. I'm pragmatic. I know figures and calculate my chances for winning or losing.'

A short laugh travels through the receiver to her ear.

'And since we are talking about figures and numbers . . .' he continues. And his tone suggests that it is no longer a laughing matter. Pragmatic, realistic, only figures and numbers: they are tangible, you can see them, no other reality exists outside them, beyond them. And while he continues to talk she tries to read the words between the lines, but there is nothing except the figures that he has added up. 'Of course, if you want to keep the baby I will be prepared to take financial responsibility.'

'And emotional responsibility?' she asks, and hears the echo of her own voice come back to her.

'Emotional responsibility? In emotional terms, I will try my best, but I can't promise anything,' he says.

He doesn't lie, he plays a fair game, he sticks to the rules. Lydia is the one who tried to cheat. She secretly marked a card in a moment he wasn't looking. He took the marked card and then coolly returned it to her. And Lydia realizes what she has to do. She has been found guilty and now she has to clean the mark off the card without anyone noticing, so that the game can continue as before, where she has nothing to lose and Claude has everything to lose. And she prays for the first time in a long while, Forgive us our sins, as we forgive those who sin against us. She doesn't know who to direct the prayer to. She thinks about Jesus, but can't make up her mind if she believes that he is the son of God.

≈

'That's not important,' says the vicar in his talk to Lydia before her confirmation. And he decides to confirm her regardless.

While Lydia thinks, But I don't believe that Jesus is the son of God, the only son of God, and she says out loud, 'How can I be confirmed if I don't believe what I am supposed to believe?'

And the vicar repeats, 'That's not important, my child.' And he confirms the girl. He is kind.

'A lovely, kind person,' says Lydia's mother. But he is not a man of God, thinks Lydia. How can he be a man of God and say, That's not important, my child, when I tell him I don't believe that God has a son. Either we are all children of God or no one is.

The Reverend Edward Bertram is sitting behind his big desk with his black collar and agrees with Lydia, and says, 'You are absolutely right, my child.'

She asks, 'What do you mean? How can I be right?'

'That we are all children of God.' Reverend Bertram nods with a good-natured, harmless sparkle in his eyes.

'So Jesus is no one special,' Lydia insists, and even to herself, her voice sounds like that of a stubborn little child. She would love to be able to express herself better, because the vicar doesn't want to understand what she is telling him.

'Jesus is the son of God, and he died for us on the Cross and he rose after three days and now he is seated at the right hand of God. And beside him no one is sitting. He is sitting there all alone. Do you understand, my child?' Reverend Bertram leans forward, pulls his big blue Bible towards him and opens it. 'I have a very good verse for you here: *Be thou faithful unto death, and I will give thee a crown of life.*' And he lifts his face and smiles at the girl. 'Do you understand, my child?'

Lydia shakes her head. 'No, I don't understand. I don't believe that Jesus is the son of God. I don't doubt that he lived,' she adds, and hopes that Reverend Bertram will be willing to discuss this. She wants to be confirmed, but only if she can believe what is right and proper.

Later this evening her mother will say, 'I met the Reverend at the butcher's. He told me you were splitting hairs.'

And her father adds, 'Leave the Reverend in peace. Confirmation is a thing one does and that's it. It's a tradition in our family.'

Lydia says to Reverend Bertram, 'I believe that Jesus lived and he was a helpful, pious man. But now he is certainly not sitting at the right hand of God, because if he was sitting there, we would all be sitting there.'

She feels her anger rise because Reverend Bertram doesn't respond. He doesn't help her to understand. All he wants to do is confirm her, despite the fact that he shouldn't be allowed to because she doesn't believe in what he tells her, what the Church tells her. Because she doesn't understand.

Then she adds, 'I don't really know if I believe in God.'

The vicar lowers his head. Lydia stares at his grey curly hair as, with his finger underneath the line of text he reads once more: '*Be thou faithful unto death, and I will give thee a crown of life.*' Then he looks at her once more, with sadness in his eyes. 'You have to believe, my child. Jesus died for us on the Cross.'

'I want to believe – honestly, you have to believe me. But I don't know how to believe. You have to help me.'

'The confirmation will help you, my child.' He looks at his watch and nods in the direction of the door. 'Your time is up. There are others waiting outside. I will see you on Sunday at church.'

They shake hands, Lydia and the vicar. And she cycles

away and at home she screams, 'The Reverend is barking mad. I will not be confirmed by him. I will not get confirmed. I don't believe in God.'

Her mother is in the kitchen baking a cake for Sunday.

'You are ungrateful,' she says. She turns back to her cake and starts pouring the mixture into the tin.

Lydia replies in a calmer voice, 'I am not ungrateful. But I simply can't believe. I would love to believe, but I don't understand it. How can Jesus be the son of God? How can he have died for all of us? That's absolute nonsense.'

Her mother has finished filling the tin.

'Do you believe?' Lydia asks.

'Believe in what?' her mother asks.

'Well, Jesus and God,' Lydia replies.

Her mother opens the oven door and pushes the cake inside.

'I was confirmed and I was grateful for the presents. I would never have dared to second guess. To scream around the house as you do. My mother wouldn't have put up with it. I am far too soft with you. I have always shown far too much leniency.'

'Now, now, you two. Don't fight.'

Her father is standing in the kitchen doorway. He is wearing his slippers and his dark-blue cardigan.

'Lydia, listen,' he says. 'As far as I am concerned, all priests and vicars have a little problem up here—' He points to his head. 'However, tradition is tradition. And it is good to be seen in church. Let Sunday come and go and no one need mention it again.'

'But you don't understand!' Lydia's voice has become shrill again. Her father is leafing through the pile of post that is lying on the sideboard. 'I can't lie,' she says. 'Especially not when it concerns God and the Church. How could I? But I don't understand how Jesus can be the son of God. Do you both believe that Jesus is the son of God?'

'Let me tell you one thing,' her mother now says in a stern voice. 'If you don't want to be confirmed we will return your new skirt and blouse to the shop. They were a lot of money.'

Her father tears open an envelope. 'In life you don't have to evaluate every single word carefully. All you have to say is that you believe in God. That's enough. That's also enough for Reverend Bertram. He understands young people. He isn't asking for much.'

'So do you believe, Dad?'

'I certainly do.'

The following Sunday Lydia is confirmed, and in the name of the Church Reverend Bertram puts a big copper cross on a woollen thread around her neck and on it is a sticker: *Be thou faithful unto death, and I will give thee a crown of life.* Revelation 2:10.

∼

And now Lydia is holding this cross and presses it against her forehead and to her lips, and whispers, 'Forgive us our sins, as we forgive those who sin against us. Forgive me my sins, dear God.' She is kneeling in St Paul's, early in the morning, before work and before the tourists flood into the cathedral.

She is sitting in St Dunstan's Chapel, to the right just after the main entrance, on a small wooden bench that is covered with red velvet. Her elbows are resting on the back of the seat in front of her. Her eyes wander from the marble pillars and the wooden wall panels to the brass chandeliers. Jesus is hovering behind the altar on a cloud with a kindly look in his eyes and his hands raised for blessing. Mary is sitting to his right and St John the Evangelist is sitting to his left. Jesus's palms are marked by the stigmata and there is a cut on his right side from which the blood still flows. Lydia folds her hands and lowers her forehead on to the copper cross between them. She is praying to God and seeking Jesus and sliding from her seat on to the floor. She is holding the cross because she has nothing else to hold on to. Her guilt and sins are increasing. Now she is playing games with life itself, making decisions over life and death. How many more sins does she want to accumulate? She feels the hard ground underneath her knees and she pulls the scarf she is wearing round her neck up over her head. If only she could become a nun. Then she wouldn't need to bother with this world any longer; she'd be in the company of other women who were walking the same path as her and she'd know it was the right path.

But Lydia can no longer become a nun because she is pregnant. She carries another life inside her, conceived in the lustful embrace of the flesh. Her flesh is lusting after Claude, so much so that she wants to feel him inside her for ever, to be united with him for ever. But he doesn't want to. He only wants her

44

body. He takes the body, satisfies his needs, then he turns away. He does not want to be bound to her, to be united, to become one for ever. It is no longer a game. It has never been a game. Because Lydia has never been capable of playing games, even as a child.

She can watch the clouds, can jump from cloud to cloud. But to play hide-and-seek with other children or go for bicycle rides or build sandcastles? Her brother and sister spend hours building sandcastles with other children. Why? They just disintegrate with the next tide. Sometimes they don't even last that long. Other children come and kick them down. She remembers at nursery sitting by the radiator watching the other children play. She doesn't want to join in. It is so nice and warm there, she feels cosy and secure. Two boys are building a Lego castle; they don't talk, they are engrossed in their game. They spend hours building something only to be able to destroy it again. Lydia can see it coming and would like to warn them, but they wouldn't understand her. And she doesn't understand them. And she can't yet actually put her thoughts into words; she only senses the nonsense of other children's games. She doesn't understand the children's senseless running around, screaming, laughing, shrieking, squealing. What's the point? And later on they will learn to play tennis, netball, cricket. And Lydia tries too. But she quickly realizes that she is not talented at any of it. She will never reach a world-class standard in any of the games or sports, she won't even win school competitions. So why should she participate? Because it is fun? But how is it supposed to be fun? She can't feel it. Why have games been invented? And by whom? Why is there a difference between games and life? She doesn't want to learn how to play games. She wants to learn about life. She watches people play cards, Monopoly, Mikado. Their seriousness, their focus, their eagerness to win. They bite their nails and twirl their hair, they can't take their eyes off the cards, off the board. They get angry, upset, fight, play on. And they all want to win. It's all about winning and losing, always. And she doesn't understand.

She should have told Claude.

And she kisses the cross in her hands and prays to Jesus, that he may come to her, that she might understand him. She looks up and sees Jesus with his kind-hearted gaze and the wounds from the crucifixion. She knows that he suffered and perhaps might still be suffering. But she also only sees a human being, the image of a human being. And she still can't believe that he has taken away all our sins.

~

It is a month before Claude calls again. He is coming to London, he needs to see her, he can't live without her. He has changed his mind, he says. He had to think things through first, but now he is sure. He wants her, he wants the baby.

'I am sorry I didn't call for a month,' he says. 'That I didn't respond to your messages, didn't answer your calls.'

That evening he rings her doorbell and stands there with thirty red roses and a bottle of Champagne in his hands. It's the first time in nearly three years that he has visited her in her bedsit. They've always met only in restaurants or his hotel.

'*Mon dieu*, how thin you are.' He steps inside. 'Shouldn't you be blooming as a mother-to-be?'

'I am no longer pregnant,' Lydia says.

'A miscarriage?' he asks.

She shakes her head. 'No.'

The door behind him is still open.

He is staring at her. Not moving. She walks past him, pushes the door shut. She doesn't want the neighbours to hear.

'You killed it. How dare you? I am a Catholic. This was my baby too.'

Lydia is still standing by the door. She looks at his massive back. 'I tricked you. The pregnancy wasn't an accident. I shouldn't have done that. I wanted to force you to stay with me. It was my baby. It had nothing to do with you.'

Claude turns around. He stares at her uncomprehendingly.

'But here I am,' he says, and he looks like a helpless little boy.

'Too late,' replies Lydia, and opens the door. 'Please leave.'

Claude takes a step forward, his arms reaching above her. She sees his movement in slow motion. He pushes the door shut, then lets his massive body slump against her, against the door.

'You little witch, you won't get rid of me that easily.'

47

He straightens up, takes her by the shoulders and shoves her hard against the door. A tearing pain shoots up her back and she sees his startled face. He lets go of her and she sinks to the ground.

'Claude, please. It's over.' Then she runs out of words.

He squats down next to her. 'Why?'

'Why are you coming only now?' she asks instead of answering his question.

'You could have waited,' he replies.

Lydia shakes her head. 'No. Today you arrived with roses, but in a few months you would have betrayed me.'

She is now leaning against the closed door. He is sitting next to her. Two children, exhausted from their game. They could be sitting together on a monkey bar. For a moment they don't speak. Lydia stares at her feet, watches how the two big toes move towards each other, touch, part. She feels her back, the pain in the back, and the hard door. She already sees herself dropping backwards from the monkey bar so that she doesn't need to observe her feet any longer – her feet that play with each other as if nothing has happened. And even though she said, 'Today you arrived with roses, but in a few months you would have betrayed me,' only becoming aware of the full implication as she spoke, because she had never seen things in such a clear and logical way before, at the very same moment she began to hope that Claude would contradict her, that he would wipe those words from her lips, that his rage would be real, that he really wanted a child with her, a family with her.

In that split second she realized that she would forgive him, she would forgive herself, if only he'd contradict her. Contradict her with force, with violence. In hate – in love – would fall on her.

But he says, 'You're right.'

And Lydia watches her feet. How they slowly form a V and then a rooftop.

~

Rafiq returns my call half an hour later. He would like to take me out to dinner tonight and he will pick me up from home at eight.

I take the afternoon off and go shopping. In the last couple of years I haven't spent much. I buy my clothes in East-end markets and I don't go out in the evenings, except to my language classes and meetings with my sisters. But now I spend. I buy make-up and hairclips and lacy underwear, a long black taffeta skirt with a matching basque. In the evening I am wearing a black blouse over the basque and a dark-grey silk hijab. I am standing in front of the mirror and studying my beautiful reflection. I open my blouse very slowly and my breasts look full and voluptuous and tempting. I hope that the meal won't estrange us. I'd love to invite him to my flat afterwards. I would have the right, because I will be his wife. I change the bed. Before he is due to arrive I pray *'isha'* – the night-time prayer. Then I put on my make-up: eyeliner and mascara. I dab my lips ever so slightly with colour I know I am allowed as a lipstick. Then I sit and wait, like a well-behaved schoolgirl on the edge of my seat with my hands folded in my lap. We have to take the marriage vows first before I get in the car with him. Otherwise I shouldn't really be in a car, in any closed space, with a man on my own. These are the rules. When at precisely eight o'clock the doorbell rings, I am startled. I tell myself to stay calm, kneel down on the floor, rest my palms on my thighs and pray one more time for God's advice. With closed eyes, I focus on my breathing, then I get up and turn off the light, close the door and walk down the stairs.

Rafiq is standing outside. He is wearing a dark blue suit and light blue shirt. The top button is open. No tie.

'*Assalam alaiki, ya* Kauthar.'

'*Wa alaik salam, ya* Rafiq.'

He is holding an open umbrella.

'Is it raining?' I ask, slightly surprised, and look up into the clear evening sky.

'No.' He shakes his head. 'But we have to take the marriage vows. And this is how my father asked my mother. Under an umbrella in the middle of Baghdad.'

I laugh and take a step forward to join Rafiq under the umbrella. We don't touch, but I can smell his aftershave and hear his breathing. I don't know if people are passing us on the pavement.

'Kauthar, I want to marry you, to be your husband for ever. But I agree to a temporary marriage on your terms for a month, so that we can get to know each other.'

A jewellery box appears in his free hand. With his thumb he pushes a small button. The lid jumps open. A gold ring with a small diamond. 'I can put it on after we exchange our vows. I am not allowed to touch you before,' he adds, almost apologetically.

I nod, and recite the words as they have been written: 'I offer you myself in marriage for a month.'

And I hear him say, '*Qabiltu*. I have accepted.'

He tucks the umbrella under his chin and pulls the ring from the little cushion. I stretch out my left arm. Rafiq touches my hand. I feel him shaking, his touch penetrates my skin, enters my hand, my arm. Spreads. Seizes my entire body. Only his touch now exists. I watch the ring glide across my knuckle. His fingers on my hand.

'It fits,' he says, barely audible, relieved.

Everything happens so easily. For a moment my hand remains in his: the contact feels unbreakable. We both look down and I know he would love to bend forward and kiss me, and I would like to kiss him too, and I know it will happen. But not now. We step apart. He closes the umbrella, offers me his arm. Slowly we walk down the quiet side street. A cab is waiting at the corner. Rafiq opens the door for me. We sit next to each other without touching, without words. I don't know this man at all. I've known him for ever.

'How often have you been married?' I ask.

'Twice.'

'Temporary marriages?'

'Yes.'

'How do you know, then, that this marriage won't be temporary too?'

'Because we stood together underneath the umbrella.'

'And with the others you didn't stand underneath the umbrella?'

'No.'

'I have never been married. But before I returned to Islam three years ago, I was with men.'

'I know.'

'How?'

'I've met Rabia's husband.'

'My friend Rabia?!' I swallow. 'But she is dead.' She died of cancer two years ago.

Rafiq nods. For a moment we are silent.

'Have you known him long?' I then ask.

'No. I met him two weeks ago. After I realized that I might have found my wife – you. Still, I wanted to be sure and I wanted to know as much as possible about you. I've asked around, discreetly of course, in order to find people who might know you. And so I met Ali, Rabia's husband. He is a lovely man. They took you into their hearts. He has only good things to say about you. And my initial hope that I had found my wife became a certainty.'

I turn my head and look out of the side window so as not to look at Rafiq, so as not to touch him. Because that more than anything else is what I want to do. But first I should ask him questions, questions that it is customary to ask. Because we are now husband and wife and we want to stay together for the rest of our lives. This decision I will take, subconsciously I have already taken it. But I will also take it consciously within the next few hours. Rafiq knows that I have a judgement to make.

'I hope you don't mind that I asked about you,' I hear Rafiq say. 'That's our custom. And moreover, I just wanted to be sure this time. I entered the other marriages carelessly, and in both instances I realized within a couple of weeks that it wouldn't work. That I had made a mistake. I have high expectations. My wife should be an intelligent, beautiful, practising Shiite. And I think I have now found her.'

'How long ago were your other marriages?'

'The first one took place when I was twenty-five and it lasted four months. The next one was two years later for six months. After that I decided to wait. And I wanted to finish my medical studies and establish myself in the profession.'

'Do you have children from these marriages?'

'No. But now I'd like some.'

'How many?'

'*Kauthar.*'

I turn my face towards him. He knows that I understand he is referring to the River of Abundance in Paradise, which also gives me my name. I would love to pull him close to me.

But not yet. The rules have to be followed. So I look out of the window again. The green of Regent's Park glides past, and two joggers.

'No, honestly. How many?'

'How many would you like? I feel that the decision about the number of children should be mainly for the woman.'

'Two,' I reply.

'I am happy with two.'

'And if it turns out to be three?'

'Then it will be three.'

'Do you prefer boys or girls?' I ask.

'That decision is with Allah. I would cherish a daughter like a princess, look after her like the apple of my eye, and help her become a wise and intelligent woman. A boy I would bring up in such a way that he can measure himself against me and hopefully overtake me one day.'

For a moment we are silent. Then I say: 'Tell me about you. Where were you born? Where did you grow up? Tell me about your studies. Your family. You know so much about me and I know so little about you.'

～

And Rafiq told me. He began in the taxi and continued in the restaurant, and then added details over the next days and weeks and months. And that evening, after our meal in the restaurant – an Iraqi restaurant, where we would eat many more times, and would also eat our last meal together in London . . . But we haven't got to that point yet. No, no, no. I want to

go back to the first evening. I want to relive it one more time.
And then I am ready to come to you. And I will love no one
else except you. I have never loved anyone except you. All the
love I have ever felt, ever experienced, was ultimately and most
importantly love for you.

I loved Rafiq like a woman loves a man, a carnal love,
and we became one for you, in praise of you. We merged our
bodies, our souls, in praise of you.

As we sat in the restaurant, we did not touch. And in the
cab on our way home we did not touch.

He opens the door of the taxi for me and while my
left hand gathers up my long skirt, my right hand lowers
itself on to his offered arm. And I say, 'I'd like you to come
upstairs.' I say it only to him, barely audible, only he can
hear me. He nods, pays the taxi and no further words cross
our lips. He follows me up the stairs. I hear his breathing,
I hear the rustling of my skirt, I hear the squeaking of
the old wooden stairs underneath the thin, worn carpet. I
unlock the door and ask him in, silently. I push the door
shut and he is standing in the small hallway. Pale-yellow
street light enters from the kitchen window. He is standing
there and waiting, because that is our agreement. These
are my terms. I am standing there and I see his hands by
his side. I know that I have all the time in the world. He
will be there and when I offer him my hand he will take
it and guide it, and we will merge, become one in praise
of Him. And we will give each other pleasure in praise of

Him. And my body is burning, consumed by desire, desire
for him and longing for Him, longing to merge, to unite,
to become one, to dissolve.

My body is being consumed by flames. I can't stop it. It is
burning, and has already burnt to ashes a long time ago, and
no one noticed how my body, my heart, my soul caught fire.
All I ever wanted was to become one with you, with you alone.
Because you are love. Only you.

We stand alone, a man and a woman, and we stand facing
each other, and we are allowed to do whatever we want to
do. God allows us because we are husband and wife. I ask
him to take a seat on the sofa in the living room. I go into
the bedroom and switch on the bedside lamp. I take off my
coat, then the hijab, let both drop on to the chair. In front of
the mirror I unbutton my blouse and let it slip over my shoulder. I lean forward and put my hand down inside the basque,
pushing my breasts up. I untie my hair and repaint my lips.
Then I walk out of the room and stand for a moment in the
doorway of the living room and his glance rests on me. And as
I walk towards him his lips move, *Bismillahir rahmanir rahim.*
In the name of Allah, the Most Merciful, the Most Kind.

~

The next morning we rise together just before dawn to perform our ablutions once again, as we did during the night.
Then for the first time in our lives we pray together the *fajr*
prayer, the first prayer of the day, which has to be recited

between dawn and sunrise. It is the first time that I pray with a man, my man. I am standing a few steps behind him, as decency demands, so that my sight does not distract him. I am wearing a white *khimar*, a cape-like veil that reaches down to the floor, covering my entire body, and only my face and hands are visible. I always wear the *khimar* for *fajr*, especially in the summer months, when the morning prayer has to be said very early, and I go back to bed afterwards. It is a practical, chaste piece of clothing and I usually wear my pyjamas underneath. But today I am naked. For a short moment, as we are standing ready for prayer, hands by our side, feet firmly planted, the prayer stones in front of us on the floor – where we will rest our foreheads during *sujud*, the prostrate position, with humility, in gratefulness – I hesitate, wondering if it is indecent to stand before God with nothing on underneath my *khimar*. But then Rafiq's voice starts rising in the call for prayer, dispersing my doubts.

And my heart is lifted up into the air, is flooded with a feeling of happiness beyond compare, is flooded with his voice, Rafiq's voice. And I start softly to follow him in prayer. Our voices join quietly, flowing together in the name of Allah, in the name of Muhammad, peace be upon him, in the name of Ali, the true successor of Allah's final prophet. For a beat I hold in my heart the twelve imams: Ali, the first, and al-Mahdi, the last, who disappeared, who was born but did not die, who is still among us and has been among us for over twelve centuries, according to our calculations here on earth. But where

he lives – there in the invisible, in the occult, in the unfathom-
able – time is calculated differently. He has lived there since a
moment ago, he has lived there since eternity. And a moment
and an eternity are one, a unit, a certainty, a truth. And Rafiq's
voice and my voice are one, our bodies are one, before God,
in the name of God, and they bow as one, as husband and
wife, before Him, the Creator to whom all praise belongs. He
created us because He loves us and so that we love Him, right
now and for ever. In the here and the now and the incomprehensible. And I feel the cold pressed earth of Karbala on my
forehead. The incomprehensible becomes tangible. And God
floods my heart. I raise my hands to my face, and with me, in
front of me, Rafiq raises his hands too. A smell of musk floods
the room and we are now in a different sphere. It is bathed in
light, and I know we are no longer here, and yet here we are,
but a here without locality. You and I, Rafiq and Kauthar, my
husband and I, my love and I, with you alone I can continue,
because of you, because with you I came here, I have arrived in
this moment. In the distance we can already recognize Jabalqa
and Jabarsa, cities built on mountains, glistening beautifully in
the sunlight, like a mirage out of nowhere, in the middle of the
desert of human existence, the desert of our earthly life, where
space and time are nothing more than servants of longing,
shadows of the eternal, infinite longing of the soul. And I hear
his voice, your voice, *Allahummaghfirlan-na*, O Allah, forgive
us and have mercy upon us and save us in this world and the
hereafter, for you are mighty above all things. *Allahu akbar*.

II

Iman – Faith

I T I S T W O o'clock in the morning and seven of them squeeze into the back of the old blue Ford. Khalid, Hussein, Muhammad, Ali, Abdullah, Majid and Rafiq. Khalid's older brother Hami, the coach, is sitting in the front next to the driver, a friend of Hami's. The other boys ride in Majid's uncle's car, a white Mercedes, imported from Germany. They do not talk, not even when they have reached the main road. They sit bolt upright with tense, serious faces. These aren't boys on their way to a football match. They are on their way to atonement, to seek forgiveness for their sins and the sins of their families, so that the gates of Paradise will stand wide open for them.

'Boys, remember the saying of our Prophet, peace be upon Him: Mourn for Imam Hussein and we will take you by the hand. So don't be ashamed of your tears. Let them flow freely.'

Hami turns, looking straight ahead again, while in the back seven heads are nodding to indicate that they have received and understood the message. Rafiq takes Khalid's hand and squeezes it. Without Khalid he would not be here. Rafiq's father has sold his life to the devil and the government, his mother is suffering because the family has to hide their religion, and his sister is interested in discos and the shortness of her skirts and nothing else. But three months ago, Khalid took Rafiq for the first time to the Mohsin mosque.

'My brother now works there as a coach for the Ashura rituals.'

At first Rafiq doesn't believe Khalid. The Ba'ath Party banned the annual Shiite mourning processions in remembrance of Imam Hussein two years ago.

Nevertheless, from now on he joins the other boys every Monday afternoon at the Mohsin mosque, while his mother believes he is at football training. He learns the lyrics of the lamentation songs by heart and learns to beat the drums. He holds the rhythm, marches in unison with the other boys while they swing and hurl the chain whips. In his imagination he sees riders, dressed in white and green, hunting through the desert on horses and camels, sees blood dripping from swords, black smoke rising from burning tents, dead bodies impaled on spears, horses without riders appearing out of a smoky haze. The Battle of Karbala. Imam Hussein is fighting alone, the sole survivor against a thousand-headed, hostile army. Rafiq is convinced he can feel in his own body the arrows that are piercing the imam. And the sword blow that eventually kills him. Imam Hussein went into this battle to die, because he knew that victory was already his, the ultimate and final victory before Allah.

And like Imam Hussein more than thirteen centuries ago, Rafiq sees himself now riding through the desert on a white horse, bent low over the animal's back, drawn sword in hand to avenge his father, his mother, his sister, Imam Hussein, Imam Ali, and all Shiites, and to fight for the end of oppression, tyranny and evil. The boy is filled with regret at not having lived during Imam Hussein's time, at not having been one of his soldiers. Because if he had lived then, he would be a hero now. But the days of heroes have gone. Today, everyone is scared, not wanting to attract attention, wanting to keep his job, his apartment, his car. But doesn't Allah love the heroes most? Rafiq wants to be loved by Allah and he wants to be a hero. The forbidden Ashura processions offer him this chance. Last year his mother didn't even allow him to be out on the street with his friends during Ashura, while his father threatened him with beatings if he even mentioned the words 'pilgrimage' and 'Karbala' in their home. That's how scared his parents are of the government and the Ba'ath Party. His parents aren't bad people. Their only fault is their fear. But he, Rafiq, their son, won't be governed by fear.

~

'Hey, Rafiq, wake up!'

Khalid nudges him. The car has stopped at the roadside

somewhere in the open between Baghdad and Karbala. The road stretches out in front of them like a black line through barren desert. Dawn is breaking. They climb out of the car; the Mercedes has parked behind the Ford. They perform their ablutions with sand, since there is no water. Then they line up behind Majid's uncle and pray. They change their clothes, taking off their vests and jeans and throwing them into the car boots. They dress in black trousers and shirts. They fasten brown belts around their waists and wind red strips of cloth around their heads. The red strips symbolize Imam Hussein's blood. To their belts they fasten the *zanjeer*, the short chain whip. They line up in rows of two. Rafiq and Khalid are, of course, standing side by side. Muhammad carries the flag, a large black banner with golden letters reading: *Ya Hussein*. Long live Hussein. Abdullah begins to beat the drum. Hami is standing bare-chested at the head of the group. He turns and nods at Khalid.

Khalid is the lead chanter and the first plaintive cry now rises from his throat: '*Ya ya karam Shiati*. O you Shiites. O you, my people.'

And everyone echoes: 'O Shiites.'

They start marching.

'O you, my noble people.'

They start beating their chests with flat hands. Right hand over left hand. Right hand over left hand.

'O Shiites. O you, my noble people!'

The sun rises and is pulled up across the sky. Rafiq's gaze

is fixed on the back of Khalid's brother, who is already beating himself with the *zanjeer*. But he is still careful not to use too much force. Karbala is far away and he has to make it.

'*Ya Ali. Ya Ali!* Long live Ali, the true leader!'

∾

They won't stop until they have reached Imam Hussein's shrine in Karbala. Six hours through the desert in the blistering heat and without water, without food. Other groups of pilgrims are now joining them. Rafiq looks up and sees a sea of countless heads before him, spread out like a huge prayer rug with an infinite number of green, black and red flags fluttering above it in the wind.

'Allah is the Greatest!'

'Long live Ali!'

'Long live Hussein!'

'Allah is the Greatest!'

'Long live Ali!'

'Long live Hussein!'

To the rhythm of the drums an unlawful, surging sea of people is rolling towards Karbala. Men in black and white *za-rouals* let the *zanjeer*, spread wide like glittering, metallic fans, slash across their naked shoulders and bare backs. Bloody red streaks begin to dance in front of eyes burning from dripping sweat. Rafiq feels sick. His dry tongue is glued to the roof of his mouth. But still he screams as loud as he can and beats his hands forcefully against his chest. He can barely wait for the blood to start flowing across his back too. He would love to pull out the chain whip right now, tear his shirt off and feel the pain, the pain that will remind him of, and link him to, the agonies suffered by Imam Ali and Imam Hussein all those hundreds of years ago. In his eyes, drops of sweat mingle with tears in anticipation of the agony that will bring him closer to Allah and Paradise. In his mind's eye he can already see the palm-lined avenue with the golden dome at the end, Imam Hussein's resting place.

But for the moment they are still on the open road, though mud huts and low, narrow houses are now lining the road. Women and children are offering water and pita bread to the pilgrims. The boys walk past without taking any. The sun has reached its zenith. They will pray *zuhr* – the midday prayer – in Karbala. Their voices have grown hoarse. Their shouting has become quieter.

Suddenly Rafiq notices a different tone in the pilgrims' cries. Aggressive, sharp sentences – at first barely audible – break through the plaintive shouts.

'*Saddam, shil idak! Shab al Iraq ma yiridak!* Saddam, get your hands off. We Iraqis don't want you. Get your hands off!'

For a moment Rafiq is confused. But Hami, who is still walking in front of them, has already joined in.

'Saddam, get your hands off!'

Rafiq sees streams of blood running down Hami's back. He hears Khalid shouting next to him: 'Saddam, we Iraqis

64

don't want you.' And then he too opens his mouth and shouts, 'Get your hands off!' Renewed energy surges through his tired body and into his arms and legs.

The men and boys are now shouting as if out of one mouth. They whip the *zanjeer* across their backs more furiously. They pull out their short knives. For a moment the metal glitters in the sun. Then the men lift the knives to their heads and cut their scalps. Blood streams down their faces.

'Saddam, get your hands off. We Iraqis don't want you. Don't want you.'

And all of a sudden Rafiq realizes that he can still become a true hero. They no longer fight against Yazin, the evil ruler in the times of Imam Hussein. Today their enemy is called Saddam Hussein. Khalid is the first of the young boys who tears off his shirt. Rafiq follows suit and pulls the chain whip from his belt. And now finally he can carve welts across his back. Welts that will prove he is a man. A tearing, burning pain drives a cowardly cry from his mouth. A sudden fright shouts through his limbs. What will Khalid think, hearing him cry like a baby because of the pain? Rafiq turns his head to look at his friend. Did he hear his cry?

But Khalid has disappeared. From behind, people are pushing against Rafiq. Khalid has been pushed forward by this powerful wave. For a second Rafiq is able to stay on his feet, but then he tumbles to the ground. The taste of sand in his mouth. He feels someone stepping on his back. He tries to get to his feet. Again he is thrown down. Someone is stepping on his leg. Only now does he comprehend what is happening. People are trampling over him, running, out of control and in panic. He manages to get to his knees, pushes himself up. Someone grabs his arm, pulls him along; a hand is clawing his upper arm. It belongs to a man with a face covered in blood. Then he lets go. And Rafiq is running, because everyone is running. He doesn't know why and he doesn't know where. He only knows that he is alone among a frenzied crowd. He has lost sight of Khalid, he has lost sight of all the other boys. He is running, because everyone is running.

The shooting, a helicopter overhead, an armoured personnel carrier. Only gradually do they sink into his consciousness. A flash here, a blast there. Then a soldier appears in front of him, pointing a gun, and fear paralyses his legs.

They put him in the back of a lorry, alongside men with bloody heads and faces and red welts on their backs. He prays that his mother and father will forgive him. At the police station he tells them his name. They take his fingerprints. He gives them his address and the name of his father. Then they put him in the cellar.

∽

And Kauthar, the Shiite from England, listens to the story of Rafiq, her husband, the Shiite from Iraq. And in her imagination she sees a gawky, black-haired boy aspiring to be a man. There he is, among the crowd of pilgrims, with a feeling in his gut that he is finally where the action is, where he will have the chance to be a hero. And that he has managed to get away from his worried, frightened mother, who in the evening still tucks him into bed with a tender kiss on the cheek.

'In the cellar I wet myself. But luckily by the time my father came to fetch me, everything had dried,' Rafiq continues. 'He used his connections to get me out quickly. On our way back to Baghdad in the car he didn't say a word. *Ya Baba*, say something. I sat next to him in the car and cried and begged him to say something, anything. But he kept quiet. When we arrived home, the first thing my mother did was to give me a slap, then, with tears of relief streaming down her face, she took me in her arms. Meanwhile, my father sat down in his chair in front of the television and started to wait. He knew what would happen. The next day he didn't go to work, nor the following. "Why is he not going to work?" I asked my mother. "He can no longer go," my mother replied. "Why can't he go any longer?" I asked. "Because of you," my sister screamed. "Because you so desperately wanted to be Shiite and revolt against the government." I knelt in front of my father and begged him to go back to work. I vowed that I would never again take part in an Ashura procession or a demonstration or go to the mosque or any assembly whatsoever. Of course, I hadn't understood anything. I thought we would soon return to normality. I apologized again and again to my father, I kissed his hands, I bathed his feet, I begged him for forgiveness.'

Rafiq pauses. He is lying on his back, his hands folded behind his head. I stroke his forehead.

'Three weeks later they came and took my father. Before they came, he forgave me. "It isn't your fault," he told me. "It all happened as it was supposed to happen." He said that Allah was punishing him because for years he had neglected his beliefs, his religion. "I want my life to be a lesson to you," he told me, "then I will not have lived and suffered in vain. Your mother, your sister and you will travel to London in a few days' time to live with Uncle Ali. Pay attention at school, don't get into trouble, study at university and build a career in a proper, decent job which will allow you to earn money and live anywhere in the world without denying your faith. Be a practising Muslim, a good Shiite. Pray and fast and trust in Allah, and when the time comes, return to your country and offer your services to your people. Be a strong man, Rafiq. Like your ancestors." Those were his words. I hear them inside my head to this day. The last words that I heard from my father. They give me strength when I tremble, they guide me and keep me on the right path. *Alhamdulillah*. Praise be to Allah.'

'What happened to your father?' I asked quietly.

'We never saw him again. Three days after they came to get him we flew to London, to my Uncle Ali. Before we travelled my father divorced my mother. He was not a weak man. I wish I could tell him that today, now that I understand. He was a very wise man. He divorced my mother so she could marry Uncle Ali in order for us to have a new home here in London. My mother cried and screamed and begged my father not to divorce her. But he insisted and said that otherwise we couldn't stay in London. She had to marry Uncle Ali in order for us to have residency and eventually become UK citizens. Uncle Ali has a British passport. My father told her that if she didn't marry him we might have problems with immigration. Also, without marriage she couldn't share the house with him. But it was my father's wish she did, so that we would be safe. My mother threw herself on the floor in front of my father, pleading with him. She wanted to stay with him – after all, she was his wife. She didn't want to marry another man, she was not a loose woman. She cried and she hit herself with the flat of her hand, on her face, on her chest, and cried and screamed and begged. My father did not change his mind. He was a strong, wise man.

'My uncle married my mother according to our laws and according to the British law at the register office. But they never shared a bed. My mother remained loyal to my father until her early death. She looked after my uncle's house and cooked and cleaned and brought up her children. He looked after us financially, as is the duty of a Muslim husband. My uncle is a good, decent man. I respect him hugely. You will meet him. You are now part of the family. And I wish I could introduce you to my father. But my father is dead. We received the message that he had died six months after our arrival here. We heard it from friends. They tortured him to death in Abu Ghraib, one of the most notorious prisons in our country. Our friends were allowed to pick up my father's body. It must have looked awful. Burn marks from cigarettes and electric cables.

My mother never knew, but I think she guessed. She never wanted to know the details. She didn't need to. But I, I wanted to know, I had to know. My father's friends told me a few years ago, once my mother had passed away. She was only fifty-one but she looked much older. Deep wrinkles marked her face and sadness had bent her back and burned her out. One night she simply slipped away, without a sound.'

~

Rafiq falls silent, and I see tears on his cheeks. I move to lie on top of him and kiss away the tears.

'We Shiites cry a lot, even men. Our hearts are heavy.' He smiles.

'Do you still have family in Iraq?' I ask.

'Only one uncle. My mother's brother. He lives in Baghdad with his wife and daughter. Fatimah, his daughter, is twenty-two. Five years ago they wanted her to marry me. But I hadn't finished my studies and didn't want to return to Iraq. And she didn't want to leave her family.'

'Would you have married her otherwise?'

'Luckily I never really had to make that decision. Uncle Ali and Fatimah's father thought about us marrying. She was seventeen then – a pretty girl, a school kid. She could never have been an equal partner for me. I pitied her, because I am aware how privileged I am to have grown up here in England, safe and well looked after, where everything was done for me, so I could learn and study and have nothing to worry about. I am aware that privilege brings responsibilities, that I have a debt and a duty towards my father and my people.'

$$\backsim$$

We are now walking across Hampstead Heath. Daisies and dandelions and chickweed in the grass. We jump across a little brook. He takes my hand again. Only an hour ago I kissed away his tears in bed, but now we are miles apart. I am walking next to a stranger, whom I trusted, thought I knew. But I suddenly realize that he too is playing games according to his own rules. *I have a debt and a duty towards my father and my people.* And these rules have nothing to do with me. He will follow them with or without me, because he followed them before he met me and he will follow them after I have gone.

We are heading up Parliament Hill. On the top a boy flies a bright-red kite.

I don't even exist as a figure on the game board. Rafiq noticed me out of the corner of his eye and thought that it might be fun to while away a moment or two with me. Soon he will turn his attention back to the game.

A gust of wind tears the kite out of the boy's hand. His game. The boy runs after the kite.

I pull my hand out of Rafiq's. I will never again watch others play games and I will never again try to play games.

'You, Kauthar, are my wife. I've searched for you all my

life. I trusted that my heart would tell me when I had found you. My heart that is guided by Allah. You ask me how you fit into the picture. Not at all. Because you are the picture. You are my life. I need you. I love you,' Rafiq says.

The red kite spirals towards the big white cumulus clouds.

∽

When our temporary marriage has come to an end, we go to the Islamic Centre. Uncle Ali is Rafiq's witness and Mr Alim is mine. The imam delivers the wedding sermon. Afterwards Rafiq carries me across the threshold and we spend a week behind closed curtains and only let go of each other to wash and pray. The world remains outside and cannot touch us. Life carries on without us, while we live a different reality. A reality of touch and union. And as I collapse on to him, and my body lies on top of his, and I hear our hearts beat together, I know that I am happy. And if I were to die at this very moment, it wouldn't matter.

∽

'The name of the first river is Pishon; it flows around the whole land of Havilah, where there is gold. The gold of that land is good; the bdellium and the onyx stone are there. The name of the second river is Gihon; it flows around the whole land of Cush. The name of the third river is Tigris; it flows east of Assyria. And the fourth river is the Euphrates.'

I stop reading and look up from the book of the Prophet Moses.

'Did you know that?' I ask Rafiq.

'No,' he replies, and leans over to me and kisses me, pulling me towards him. 'That's precisely why I married you. You are clever and you will show me the way to Paradise.'

∽

We move into the top flat of an old Victorian house close to the hospital where Rafiq works and with a view across Islington.

∽

Rafiq says, 'You don't have to work. As your husband I should look after you. Use the time to finish your Arabic studies.'

I continue working three days a week. My Arabic improves quickly. We now often talk in Arabic rather than English. I start wearing more colourful skirts, sometimes even with a pattern. We go for afternoon strolls on the Heath, hand in hand. The autumn sun filters through the red and yellow leaves and we walk through the rays. A young couple in love. In the evenings we eat dinner by candlelight. I buy evening dresses, nice underwear to surprise Rafiq.

I have found my way, my religion, my husband, my life.

∽

And she bows to God in prayer. And she bends over her husband in love and lust. And she is ready to conceive a new life inside her. And she waits. And the waiting is still quiet. In the packed Tube as she travels to work she sees pregnant women every morning. Women who proudly show off their bellies. She feels a faint tearing inside her, beneath her abdominal wall. Her skin tightens, pulls as if she were the pregnant woman. The months pass. December, January. Soon it is spring, then summer. She asks God for patience. Allah rewards the patient one. She is thinking about the first pregnancy and asks Him for forgiveness. She hasn't told Rafiq. Perhaps she should, so that no secret stands between them. Perhaps it is this secret that still divides them, prevents them from a true union. God knows and is giving her a sign.

~

I tell Rafiq and he takes me into his arms.

'You are a different person now to how you were back then. Your path to Allah was difficult. But you have arrived and Allah has forgiven you, so I must and can forgive you too.'

He enters me and afterwards kisses my tummy.

'Maybe this might help,' he says.

We both laugh and pull the blanket above our heads.

'Are you referring to the kiss or the other bit?' I tease him, and take his head between my hands, and pull him up towards me and tousle his wiry, curly, short hair. The date is

23 *Jumaada al-thaany* 1422. I don't work Tuesdays and Rafiq has worked the night from Monday to Tuesday. The date is 11 September 2001 and no secret stands between Rafiq and me.

≈

The telephone rings and Rafiq says, 'Let's not answer.' My hand glides from his shoulder blades down to the dent at his coccyx. He breathes into me and I feel his and my wetness. Uncle Ali's voice speaks on the answer machine in the living room. For a split second we both listen. We can't decipher the words. The voice stops and once again we are alone. Eventually, however, we have to leave the bed, to wash, to pray, to eat. As I am in the bathroom, I hear Uncle Ali's voice again. He is talking in English, judging by the intonation and melody of his voice. He is doing this for my benefit, because I still struggle to understand fluent Arabic when I can't see the speaker face to face.

'What did your uncle want?' I ask, walking into the living room.

Rafiq shrugs his shoulders. 'He just said we should call him back.'

Rafiq takes a bath. I blow-dry my hair. We pray *asr* and *maghrib* together – the late-afternoon and after-sunset prayers. Rafiq prays some more, to catch up with the prayers he missed while at work. I am standing in the kitchen, preparing an omelette, when Rafiq comes in and says that we should head to his uncle's, he insists that we watch the news on television. We don't have a television. Rafiq's arm reaches out over my shoulder and he turns on the radio that stands on the windowsill.

I ask, 'What's happened?'

The onion on the chopping board falls into beautiful slices underneath the sharp kitchen knife.

'The United States of America has been attacked,' declares George Bush on the radio. As if he had waited for my question. I put down the knife and look at Rafiq questioningly, wondering if he can explain. Bush's voice, news reporters, background noise from America. I move the frying pan on the gas flame back and forth, then I push a wooden spoon underneath the omelette and turn it in one quick movement. Twin Towers, hijacked planes flying into the towers, towards the Capital. Wailing of sirens from America. Screaming. *Oh, my God, it's falling it's falling the North Tower is falling.*

'Why is no one mentioning the people?' I ask. 'Surely people must have died,' I say, as if what is happening is already in the past, concluded, finished. An end, not a beginning.

'We have to go to my uncle's,' Rafiq urges.

He orders a minicab. I put on my hijab. In the taxi the radio plays, a miniature Quran dangles from the rear-view mirror. I hold the basket with the omelette and the half-finished salad on my knees. The Twin Towers are collapsing. 'They are jumping,' screams a voice. 'Jeez, they are jumping.' The cab stops, I open the door, get out. From the corner of my eye I watch Rafiq bending forward to hand the driver a banknote. He refuses.

'*Allahu akbar*, my brother. Allah is the Greatest. Today is a glorious day. America is being attacked. Today I don't take money from brothers.'

I am now standing on the pavement. I turn around and see Rafiq's face from the side, his mouth a thin, tense line.

'Take the money,' he hisses.

'*Allahu akbar*,' the driver repeats.

Rafiq opens his hand, the note drops down on to the passenger seat. Without another word he leaves the car, walks around it, towards me, touches my arm.

'Let's go.'

~

Later, I watch the images of the towers that collapse as if made of cardboard and people falling out of them – little figures drawn by children playing hangman. The name – Osama bin Laden – at some point someone mentions him. I've heard the name before, perhaps two or three times.

'Do you think the driver knew more than he let on?' I ask Rafiq as we are lying in bed in the dark next to each other, my left hand in Rafiq's right.

'No. He simply enjoyed the idea that America has been hit.'

'And you? Do you enjoy the idea?' I ask.

'No. Of course not. Murder doesn't solve anything.'

'But American soldiers stood by and watched Saddam

Hussein's soldiers slaughtering thousands of innocent Shiites, among them some of your family,' I say, my heart reaching out to those slaughtered in the south of Iraq by Hussein's men as they withdrew from Kuwait after the Gulf War.

'America has done a lot of damage in Iraq. Saddam Hussein too. And also the Iraqi people themselves,' Rafiq replies. Then he places a kiss on my forehead. 'Let's sleep. Goodnight, *habibi*.'

I lie awake for a long time. I see the planes, the towers, the people, and hear the screaming desperation, the dumb-founded panic, because suddenly a game is being played with rules that no one understands. In my mind I see men and women who a few hours ago were heading to work. And then with no warning war breaks out and the innocent masses are dying. The innocent masses who just wanted to earn their daily bread. It's always the innocents who die, little figures drawn by children playing hangman. And these little figures are jumping to their death on our TV screens.

But we never witness them hitting the ground.

Rafiq breathes calmly and steadily. I pull my hand from underneath the blanket and stroke the back of his head gently. I am crying. I wish the world could be a better place. Then Rafiq wouldn't need to escape into sleep. Then no one would need to try to escape without any chance of succeeding.

The early-morning prayer eases the weight on my heart. I concentrate on the words, the movements, my rhythm, Allah's rhythm. As my forehead rests on the prayer stone, I once again know that God will hold me. Rafiq goes back to bed after the prayer. He is on a late shift. I am standing at the window in the kitchen, holding a mug of coffee between my hands. I gaze across the open expanse that slants southwards down into the valley of London. The day is dawning, but the darkness of night is still hanging in the air. It will be a bright and clear day. Autumn is still being held at bay. I could go for a walk on the Heath. I could hope that Rafiq follows me, to comfort me, protect me. To lead me away to somewhere else. Because here things have changed, and they will never be the same again.

~

On the Tube everyone is hiding behind newspapers. Me too. At work I hear myself say a few times, 'They weren't Muslims. Not true Muslims. They call themselves Muslims, like bin Laden calls himself a Muslim. But terrorism is not part of Islam. What happened in America is terrorism, not jihad. Jihad describes the personal struggle to lead a godly life. You have to fight the devil within you. Muhammad, peace be upon Him, said that the inner jihad is the greater jihad.'

My colleagues are listening to me. They want to learn, they want to understand; they know I am a good Muslim. But they also pity me. After all, hasn't the world suspected for quite a while now – at least since Khomeini – that Islam is an aggressive religion? And this is the final proof. They are attacking innocent people in America. They, the Muslims, with their jihad, their holy war, they are attacking the West. And they justify their aggression with their religion. And you, Kauthar, still deny everything, say, No, that's not true, Islam is a religion of the middle path. As a Muslim you are allowed to defend yourself if you are being attacked. You do not need to turn the other cheek. But the right to self-defence does not lead to terrorism.

I suddenly have to justify myself, as if I have committed an atrocity. My colleagues nod their heads in sympathy, while their eyes betray doubt. Well, there must be something that this woman simply doesn't understand in her naivety. Perhaps she doesn't want to understand. And I shake my head and make for home. I leave the train, take the escalator up, pass the ticket barrier, exit straight ahead as usual. I climb the stairs to street level. I pass the newspaper kiosk and McDonald's. Outside the pub a group of drunken men linger. I keep my head lowered, my eyes fixed on the pavement in front of my feet.

'Fucking cunt,' I hear, but don't think they are addressing me.

'We'll fuckin' show ya.'

Something wet hits my left cheek. I don't stop, continue walking. My hand on my cheek. When I finally take it away spit is stuck between my fingers. I climb the hill, pass the hospital. I could go in and ask for Rafiq. But he might be – in fact, he will be – busy. If he is busy I would need to wait, I'd stand there and I would start to cry. I can't do that. I want to get home to clean myself. To be alone, to hold myself in a pose that is worthy of Him, so that He will hold me, so that I don't

80

fall apart. I wipe my cheek with the sleeve of my cardigan. I rub my face as I walk, my glance fixed to the grey asphalt. I pull the hijab further over my forehead and across my cheeks. It was only a bit of spit, it can be washed away. As soon as the door falls into its lock behind me, I tear the hijab off my head and my cardigan off my body. I let both items drop to the floor. Perhaps I should throw them away immediately. They can't be used again. Perhaps it's enough to wash them. Why not? It's only someone else's saliva. I don't know what to do with the clothes. Can't think straight at the moment. I scrub my hands and wash my face with ice-cold water, rubbing until they turn bright red. I close the curtains. I don't want anyone to see me, anyone to know that I am here. I have washed my hands and face but haven't yet performed the ritual cleansing obligatory before addressing God in prayer. Nevertheless I take the prayer stone and put it on the floor. I kneel down and bow and put my forehead on the cold stone. And hope that Allah will forgive me for not cleaning myself properly and not performing the prayer correctly. Not yet. I will fulfil my duties later. I want to lie here and feel God's breath inside me.

Eventually everything around me becomes quiet. I thank God that He has let me lie here, that He isn't angry with me. I get up and prepare myself for prayer, performing *wudu'*, the ritual cleansing. Then I pray *maghrib* and *'isha'* – the end-of-day and night-time prayer – together. I pray for a long time. I pray four additional units. I let Allah's name resound inside me, until He fills me and pain and sorrow disappear from my heart. Rafiq won't come home before ten or ten thirty. I prepare a soup that we will eat later. I am infinitely rich and lucky because I have Allah, who shows me the right path. And I pity the poor drunken men, who are lost in the darkness and spit in my face out of fear.

~

When the phone rings I contemplate not answering for a moment. But then I lift the receiver just before the answer machine switches itself on.

'Lydia?'

'Mum.'

'My God, have you seen the news from America? Isn't it awful? How can anyone do this? I am so shocked. I've been glued to the telly all day. Innocent people . . . you know they are innocent people.'

'Yes, it is awful,' I say calmly.

My voice comes from far away. I sit down on the sofa – sit next to myself, next to the woman who is holding the receiver. She is only an empty shell, hollow from the inside. My mother's words fall into this hollowness, where they vanish without trace.

'How is such hatred possible? How can anyone hate someone else so much?' she says.

I am waiting, not sure yet where she is heading with her lamentation. Will she, too, hold me responsible for what is happening in America? I hear her sobbing.

'I am totally at the end of my tether. Life is so cruel. People are so cruel. This hatred, this violence nowadays.'

Then suddenly she stops. Only to ask in the next second in a sharp, high-pitched voice, 'Are you still wearing the scarf around your head?'

'Of course. It's part of my faith.'

'Lydia, that's not religion. That's some barbaric ritual. Distorted. Deluded. Religious belief is connected to the desire for peace. What these Muslims are doing is prehistoric, barbaric. When will you finally come to your senses? Are you proud of what's happening in America?'

'No, I am not proud. What's happening in America is a criminal act, it's terrorism. And terrorism is not part of Islam. They abuse Islam, misinterpret it—'

I want to continue speaking but my mother interrupts me. 'I didn't even dare to go out on to the street today. I was so frightened.'

'Why?'

'I am frightened that neighbours and people I know might stop me in the street and ask about you. If you approve of what is happening in America. What should I reply?'

'That I don't approve, of course. You surely can't doubt that.'

'Not doubt? Are you surprised? Running around with a scarf over your head? Everyone knows it. You announced it to the entire world. Luckily, I haven't told a soul that you got married to one of these Muslims, these Arabs. I can't deal with their faces. And can anyone blame me?'

Anger starts welling up inside me. I don't want it to reach my mouth. I don't want to shout at my mother. It wouldn't change anything. I need to finish this conversation.

Dear Dad,

I am writing this letter to you. Mum, however, can read it too. In fact I want her to read it. But I'd like you to be there with her and explain to her things she might not understand. I love and honour you both and never wanted to hurt you in any way. I know how difficult it is for you to accept that I am a Muslim. But this is my path and there is no other path for me. Only now, in retrospect, do I understand that my experiences as a child, teenager and young adult have always pointed in this direction. I am grateful that you gave me a home and offered me shelter while I was small and helpless. My gratefulness is immense and God knows it. Now I am walking along my path and I realize that by doing so I am hurting Mum. I don't want to hurt her, or you. All I want is for you to accept the path I have chosen, for you to accept me as a Muslim.

Over the last few years, I have tried to explain my beliefs to you. I will now try again.

The attacks in America have shocked the world, the East as much as the West, Muslims as much as Christians, me as much as you. The men who committed these crimes call themselves Muslims, just like

84

Osama bin Laden and his al-Qaeda consider them-selves to be Muslims. But, as I've already said to Mum on the phone, they are not Muslims. They are terrorists who don't know their own religion and they turn and twist the words until it suits their own purpose.

You are to devour all the nations which the LORD your God is giving over to you. Show none of them mercy, so that you do not serve their gods; that is the snare which awaits you.

When you advance on a town to attack it, make an offer of peace. If the offer is accepted and the town opens its gates to you, then all the people who live there are to be put to forced labour and work for you. If the town does not make peace with you but gives battle, you are to lay siege to it and, when the LORD your God delivers it into your hands, put every male in it to the sword; but you may take the women, the dependants, and the livestock for yourselves, and plunder everything else in town. You may enjoy the use of the spoil from your enemies which the LORD your God gives you.

These quotes are from the Bible, Deuteronomy.

Why do I quote the Bible, if we actually want to talk about Islam? To show you from the start that neither the Bible nor the Holy Quran deals exclusively with love and compassion. Both books are filled with descriptions of violence.

However, do these biblical commands, as I quoted them, mean that Jews and Christians are supposed to act upon them in our times? No. Most Jews and Christians – those by name and those who actively follow their religion – would argue that such texts need to be seen in a historical context. *Six days shall work be done, but on the seventh day there shall be to you an holy day, a sabbath of rest to the LORD: whosoever doeth work therein shall be put to death.* No one would any longer take this quote out of context and argue for slavery or the death penalty for someone who has worked on the Sabbath. But of course, let's be clear, there might be some who do.

Islam commands jihad. But jihad should not be translated as 'holy war'. Holy war is a concept rooted in Western Christian civilization that probably stems from the time of the Crusades. To translate 'jihad' as holy war or religious war is wrong and misleading. But this misinterpretation is deeply engrained in our culture. Even in my Arabic–English dictionary it states: 'fight, battle; jihad, holy war (against the infidels, as a religious duty)'. These words are a scandal – and reveal the ignorance of our culture and language towards Islam.

The root of jihad is *ja-ha-da*, which means 'to endeavour, strive, labour, take pains, put oneself out; to overwork, overtax, fatigue, exhaust'. The Holy

Quran says: *jahada fi sabil Allah*. *Fi* translated by itself means 'in' and *sabil* means 'path, way'. So *jahada fi sabil Allah* translated literally is 'to strive/labour/take pains in the way/in the path of God'. In other words, to make a big effort in order to follow the path of God. *Jahada* and its noun jihad carry no implication of violence. Both words refer to the inner struggle to be closer to God. And in the Holy Quran there are frequent exhortations to exert ourselves for God and not cling to worldly possessions. This, however, does not imply killing oneself or others. We are commanded to work on ourselves, to be selfless, less selfish, to do good, to help people in need.

But I will not lie to you, there is another expression in the Quran, very similar, that differs in one significant word: *qatala fi sabil Allah*. And *qatala* means 'to kill', even though often this word is translated as 'to fight'. To kill in the way of God, for the sake of God. 'And kill/fight in the way of Allah those who kill/fight you.' 'And kill/fight them wherever you meet them.' 'And the one who fights (*qatala* – kills) in the way of Allah, may he be killed or win, we will give him an immense price.' So are we Muslims commanded to kill? No. Because the Quran also says: 'Fight (*qatala* – kill) in the way of Allah those who fight (*qatala* – kill) you but do not transgress. Indeed Allah does not love transgressors.'

'But do not transgress!' In other words, only if

someone is attacking you and is about to kill you, are you then allowed to defend yourself.

God's love is a precondition for our human love for Him. *He loves them and they love Him.* A famous verse in the fifth Sura. He has to love us; only then can we love Him. If, however, we transgress His laws, He will banish us and the way to Him will be closed. Faithful Muslims do everything within their power to keep this path open. We are not allowed to commit crimes.

With love,

Your daughter Kauthar

~

Dear Lydia,

When your letter dropped through our letter box, we couldn't wait to open it. It is so rare to receive letters from you. I have not much to say, except that you know our door is always open to you.

Mum

PS I too send you much love. Dad

~

I see her! I see Rabia as I push open the door. She is standing at the sink and has removed her headscarf. Her feet are bare inside her sandals. She usually wears black socks. Her long, thick, grey hair is in a plait at the back. She pulls the wedding ring off her finger and places it on the side of the sink. I hesitate for a moment. Should I say hello or would I be disturbing her preparation for prayer? Our eyes meet in the large mirror above the sink. I greet her with a nod. She was born in the same year and town as my mother. I logged her registration into the computer when she first joined the library. She comes twice a week to work on her PhD thesis. I don't sneak after her but when I pass her desk or meet her among the bookshelves, I glance at her surreptitiously. She always wears dark colours – dark brown, dark blue, dark grey or black. Long, coat-like dresses down to her ankles – sometimes they touch the ground; long sleeves, which even now in the summer she never pushes up. She wears her headscarf pulled over her forehead, folded inwards at the sides by her temples, then down underneath her chin and fastened with a pin on the right side at the height of her cheekbone. The scarf falls in a triangle halfway down her back and covers her chest completely. Her skin is beautifully clear and clean, like that of a young woman, and her face is always calm. Whatever she does – searching for books on the shelves, typing on her laptop or washing in preparation for prayer, she seems to focus and concentrate on the task at hand.

I've turned on the tap and water runs over my hands. They are shaking. The alcohol from last night is still in my blood. I am drinking too much. Each night a bottle. And since I turned thirty the drinking has started to take its toll. From the corner of my eye I observe Rabia.

She puts her right hand underneath the thin stream of water, the palm cupped to catch some of the liquid, which she then pours into the palm of her left hand. She turns the right elbow outwards and leans slightly forward over the sink. The water is now running down her elbow and lower arm. Her left hand strokes twice from her right elbow all the way to the end of her fingertips. I look away, rubbing soap into my hands. I don't want to spy on her, it must be embarrassing for her. It is embarrassing for me.

But the next moment I stare again, spellbound, and can't avert my eyes, like a child who has spotted something beautiful and wants to copy it.

I turn off the tap and shake water from my hands forcefully as proof that I actually don't care, that I have my own business to attend to. I turn around and walk past Rabia's back to the dryers on the wall. While the hot air is blowing I stare out of the window down into the small, shadowy back yard. Then I lift my eyes to the black tarred roof terrace surrounded by black railings on the opposite side. I hear a helicopter. Rabia is now parting her hair. She slowly draws a line with the three middle fingers of her right hand from the top of her head across her face down to her chin. She bends forward. She has slipped out of her shoes. She places the middle finger of her right hand between her big toe and the long toe of her right foot and then strokes with her palm upwards across the instep. She repeats the movement along the left foot. I see every detail. Her actions are slow and controlled, a perfect little performance undertaken by herself for herself. She straightens up, lifts her head and catches my glance in the mirror. She smiles. Instinctively I want to turn away, pretending that all the while I have been drying my hands, with my thoughts elsewhere.

And then, as I have already started to turn, I stop. And return her glance in the mirror.

'Hello,' I say with a smile.

She returns my greeting. We chat briefly. I tell her that I am working at the library, she tells me that she is working on a PhD thesis. She picks up her wedding ring and slides it on to her finger. Then she starts putting her headscarf back on.

'I'd love to talk to you about your religion one day,' I say, and my heart begins to race as if I am scared that she will deny me that wish.

'With pleasure,' she replies.

The following day she is not in the library. In my break I linger by the shelves with the books on Islam and pull one out every now and again, all the while listening for my colleagues. I don't want anyone to see me looking at books about Islam. That's also the reason why I can't borrow them. If it were books about Buddhism, Hinduism or even Judaism, it wouldn't matter. But Islam is different. On Saturday I go to Edgware Road. In an Islamic bookshop I buy a Quran and an introduction to Islam. I stuff the plastic bag containing the books into my shoulder bag and don't even dare to take them out in the underground because someone I know might see me. At home I leaf through the Quran as if it's any odd book, study the prayer position in the introduction, imitate the movements and remain on my knees with my forehead on the floor. It reminds me of the child position in yoga. I enjoy being on my knees, with my forehead touching the floor, hands by the side of my thighs. The deep breathing calms me and I can imagine that it must be good for anyone to perform these movements a few times a day. The prayers in the book are in Arabic, with English translation and transliteration. I repeat the first two words aloud, *Allahu akbar*. Allah is the Greatest. The Arabic letters resemble beautifully drawn loops. Chaos at first. Only after further scrutiny does the perfect, sublime order becomes apparent. I try to copy the letters on a piece of paper, drawing first from left to right until I remember that Arabic is written from right to left. As a child I spent hours copying stories from magazines. I decorated unblemished white paper with entwining flourishes. And now, as I try to draw Arabic words for the first time, I remember how important and meaningful my work appeared to me back then. How I lived in the moment of seeing the pen travelling across the paper. How I lost myself in the drawing. Even today, when I speak on the phone or sit alone at my kitchen table in the evenings, drunk, I paint letters, ideally with a fountain pen. Lines in wet ink, entwined, decorative ornaments, patterns that start off with a letter, then slowly turn into chaos – or so it appears – the more loops and hoops, twirls and twists I develop from that letter in one unbroken line, without ever lifting my pen. Until suddenly the line returns to complete the letter. From there it moves on to the next letter and a word appears.

And while I copy Arabic words, the meaning of which I do not yet understand, I think how beautiful it must be to start all over again like a small child. To stumble with wide-open eyes into a knowledge that before was closed off. Arabic is not only a foreign language like German or French. It's a different script, an unfamiliar way of thinking, another religion and culture, new laws and rules that I would have to learn like a newborn.

In a few weeks' time I will ask Rabia if it is permitted in Islam to make mistakes, and she will reply, 'Of course. After all, making mistakes is only human. What counts in Islam is the intention, and as long as your intention is good and proper and towards God, mistakes are permissible and you will be forgiven and you will learn.'

Now I am sitting at my table and I am again drinking wine, even though I didn't want to, and I am drawing Arabic twirls, and I imagine that I will convert to Islam just because I love to draw beautiful Arabic twirls, and I want to learn to draw them properly. Of course I would have to give up the wine. But wouldn't I be happy to do that? Wouldn't it be wonderful to lose myself like a child without the influence of alcohol in the painting of letters and words? And I stop drawing and look at the pictures of the ablution before prayer. But without a body performing in front of me, these images are meaningless. I start to read. *Islam* is the Arabic word for submission and devotion, the belief in one God and His Prophet Muhammad. Muhammad was the final messenger. Before Muhammad there were other messengers, among them Adam, Abraham, Moses, David, Solomon and Jesus.

Rabia will explain to me: 'We believe in Jesus, peace be upon him. We also believe in the Ascension. But we don't believe that Jesus was crucified or that he was the son of God. The Quran states clearly that God has no son and no daughter. *Say, He is Allah, the One. Allah is Eternal and Absolute. He neither begets nor is He born, and there is none like Him.* This is what it says in the 112th Sura, Al-Ikhlas, the Sura of Sincerity, which we recite each day in our prayers. And because He is One, He cannot be divided. And that's why we consider belief in a holy trinity to be a sin. That is the single big difference to Christianity.'

'And what happens to the original sin? From which Jesus is supposed to have saved us through his crucifixion?'

'In Islam we believe that each of us possesses a personal relationship with God. We don't need an intermediary. Allah forgives us our sins in the very moment we turn towards Him and ask Him for forgiveness. When we convert to Islam, when we embrace the act of submission and devotion to God, we are saved and delivered from evil and will be returned to Paradise.'

~

Rabia teaches me how to pray, and I now pray at home in the evenings, but never in the mornings. And I only wear the hijab when I meet up with Rabia and her friends – before I head down into the Tube I have already taken it off. And I am still drinking wine and I am still not thinking about what I eat. But I am increasingly aware that I am not paying attention to what I put into my mouth, and that if I were a Muslim I would need to pay attention.

One day we are sitting side by side in the bus, Rabia and I, and I am wearing a long skirt and a wide, long-sleeved blouse, both of which I always wear when I meet her to see what it feels like – I think it feels very feminine – and she suddenly says to me, 'You know, when I was a teenager and in my early twenties, before I returned to Islam – because we Muslims believe that we are all born as Muslims and as such the conversion to Islam means a return – I was convinced that I had to fight for my happiness, for my peace of mind, for my independence. But the moment I submitted to Islam, I realized how wrong I had been. The complete opposite was the case. I didn't need to fight, to be defensive, aggressive, tear myself away. Instead I had to accept, to submit. To serve Allah. And as long as I serve Allah I am free, I have peace of mind, and know precisely in each minute of my life what to do.'

~

And she throws her head back, laughing. She opens her mouth, and she will talk, and she will give me answers, answers that I will recognize, that will show me the path beneath my feet. The path I am already on but that I have only now become aware of. I will stumble and fall, but I won't remain on the ground. I will get up and continue on my way.

∼

Rabia and I visit Istanbul and we pray in the old mosques. We walk miles to the Fatih mosque, to the Eyüp Sultan mosque. We cross the Bosphorus to the Asian side and visit the Atik Valide mosque. We enjoy the peace and quiet in the small mosques, sitting on the soft carpets while a breeze gently caresses us. Rabia shows me how to use the prayer beads. Thirty-four times *Allahu akbar* – Allah is the Greatest. Thirty-three times *Alhamdulillah* – All praise is for Allah. Thirty-three times *Subhan Allah* – Glory to God. The words are no longer unfamiliar. Remembering them is easy now. Allah's praise comes to my lips as if I had been born with this knowledge. In the past months I have learned more than ever before in my life. A new world has opened up to me, a new understanding that I can now grasp but to which I was blind and deaf until a few months ago. I was not ready to conceive it then, but now I have arrived – amazed, hungry, eager.

∼

And when I am lost and don't know what to do, I can ask Rabia, my patient friend. She teaches me to enter a mosque or a room with the right foot first, but the bathroom with the left.

She teaches me which parts of the prayers are obligatory and which earn you special merit. She teaches me the difference between partial ablution, and when it is permitted, and full-body ablution. She tells me not to wear nail varnish or make-up when praying, not to use perfume that contains alcohol, and that everything I do should be done with the intention of getting closer to God. My day now has a structure, a scaffolding. I imagine a parallel beam along which I can walk, a step at a time, across the day. I won't slip, I can't slip. The five prayers are the most important part of my day, giving it content, dignity, purpose. Because every day I serve Allah, and I know what to do and how to do it. When doubts assail me, I go to Rabia.

At the beginning I fear the doubts, worried that they could destroy my belief, that they are proof that I am an impostor, a hypocrite. And each time Rabia wipes away my doubts: 'Be patient. Indeed Allah is with the patient.'

And I ask Rabia, 'Isn't Islam misogynistic?'

'For Allah there is no difference between the soul of a man and the soul of a woman. We are all from Him and we will all return to Him. *O mankind! Be careful of your duty to your Lord Who created you from a single soul and from it created its mate and from them twain hath spread abroad a multitude of men and women.* However, there is a physical difference between men and women. And Islam and we Muslims accept and acknowledge this difference in our earthly appearance. But these differences are not meant to put one above the other. They are there so we complement each other. Girls and women – just like boys and men – have to learn, have to acquire knowledge. According to Islam, it is not allowed to marry them off against their will, they have a right to divorce, to their own wealth, to political decisions.'

'Then why do Muslim women cover themselves? Wear a hijab?'

'*O Prophet! Tell thy wives and thy daughters and the women of the believers to draw their cloaks round them. So that they may be recognized and not annoyed.* It really depends who you want to serve. We all have to serve, that's part of being human. We can't escape it. And I serve God. Allah. The hijab is a sign of my service to Allah. It indicates that part of me that belongs to Allah, and only to Allah, not to this world.'

~

And I submit to Allah and to His laws and step outside wearing a hijab. And it appears as if I am covering myself, hiding behind a veil. But in actual fact I am revealing my true self. My self that can now glimpse the light.

III

Harb – War

AFTER THE LETTER from my parents, I start wearing a cloak – an *abaya* – whenever I leave our flat. It makes me feel safe.

The war in Afghanistan and the expectation of war in Iraq fill the air. Premonitions that with each day race closer towards certainty. To start with, a rumbling beneath the surface can be heard, the ground under my feet begins to shift, still there but no longer fixed, a tiny movement at first, a millimetre or two, hardly noticeable. Almost a misapprehension, a flicker in the eye. The imagination playing games. But no, no games. This time we are not playing games. But Lydia – why is she back? Why has Lydia turned up again? I am Kauthar. Only because my mother insists that I am Lydia. Whatever. If she insists, let her. It's got nothing to do with me. With Kauthar. But still, Lydia has turned up again. I know that it is Lydia who once again has understood nothing. Absolutely nothing. However, as always, she is convinced that she has understood everything. That she knows it all. And she nods with pride and satisfaction: it is all only a game. Saddam Hussein and weapons of mass destruction? A nice game, a funny game. Even Lydia gets it. A game with Bush and Blair as cartoon characters leading the way.

Rafiq says, 'They mean what they say. They will go to war in Iraq.'

Lydia strokes his head, strokes the head of my husband. I know it is her. She has crept back and now sits between us.

'No, no. Don't be silly. They won't attack Iraq.'

Rafiq suddenly stands up. Lydia's hand slides from his head and falls on to the sofa.

'Don't be so naive,' he says, and walks out of the room.

The door to the bedroom falls shut behind him. A few moments later it opens again. And Lydia, poor Lydia, is still sitting on the sofa, in the half-dark. She hasn't moved, doesn't move, while Rafiq puts on his jacket in the hallway.

'Where are you going?' asks Kauthar.

'To Ahmed,' replies Rafiq. 'We Iraqis have to stick together. I'll be back late. Don't wait up for me.'

Later she feels him coming to bed. She is lying on her side, still awake. But doesn't stir. He moves closer.

'Kauthar?' he whispers.

She hesitates. Should she pretend to be asleep?

'Kauthar, are you asleep?'

Then she replies, because she is lonely, and playing games is not her thing.

'No.'

'I am sorry I said that you were naive.' He puts an arm around her from behind.

'Do you think there will be war?' she asks into the dark.

'Yes.'

'And your friends, do they think so too?'

'Yes.'

She turns on to her back. They are now lying next to each other. Their arms touch but they don't link hands.

'I am pregnant,' she says into the night. Kauthar says into the night. I say into the night. And I feel Rafiq's face suddenly hover above mine, planting kisses on my forehead, my nose, my cheeks, my lips.

'*Alhamdulillah!* Praise to God. What wonderful news. Why are you only telling me now?'

'I did a test this morning, but I wanted to wait to do it again. It's positive. Twice.'

He kisses me once more. '*Alhamdulillah*. I started worrying that we might not be able to have children at all. But I always thought I had to leave it up to you to raise the subject.'

I am still lying on my back. I haven't moved. Arms by my side.

'Kauthar, *habibi*, what's the matter? Aren't you happy?'

'I am afraid. What will happen to us if a war breaks out?'

'What will happen? We are a proper family now.'

'"We Iraqis have to stick together", that's what you said when you went to Ahmed's earlier on. That didn't include me. I am not an Iraqi.'

'I didn't want to exclude you. I'm under quite a lot of pressure at the moment and sometimes say things I don't mean. Iraq will need us one day – you and me and our children. Here, we merely try to survive. We don't belong here.'

~

Two months later they bomb Baghdad. Circles of light flicker across the TV screen. Explode. Little toy bombs. They hit me in the stomach like real ammunition. I bend forward. I have to protect my baby, our baby, Rafiq and Kauthar's baby. How is it possible that this can just happen and no one puts an end to it? Why did no one prevent it? No one seems to say, Well, this simply isn't possible. Because in actual fact it is possible. Look at the screen. Look at what the cameras are seeing. And Kauthar is sitting in front of the screen – they have bought a TV. She is watching the news, like a movie, a war movie, and she thinks she is hit. But we can't just drop bombs and then insist that nothing, absolutely nothing, has happened. Clinical precision. No one wounded. No one dead. Only heroes. And Kauthar feels Rafiq's hand. She would love to hold on to it. A tangible reality. He withdraws his hand in order to pick up the phone, again and again he tries to get through to Iraq, to his friends, his relatives. But there is no connection.

~

The phone rings. Rafiq picks up, then hands me the receiver.

'Lydia?'

'Mum.'

'I've been trying to get through to you for hours. Always engaged.'

My mother doesn't like ringing my mobile.

'Rafiq is trying to get through to his people in Iraq.'

'Does he know people there?'

'Of course. He comes from there. He's got family, relatives and friends there. You know that.'

'How awful.'

'Mum, I really can't talk for long now. Rafiq would like to keep the line free in case someone from home calls.'

'I'm going into hospital tomorrow for an operation.'

'What?'

'I have a tumour.'

I feel the receiver in my hand and I feel myself swallow.

'What sort of tumour?'

'Dad said I shouldn't tell you. You have enough worries about the war and you probably take it personally – the war, I mean – because you are now a Muslim.'

'What sort of tumour?' I repeat.

'They say it's been growing for a while. And they also say the operation will be fine. But operations are always risky. Especially at my age.'

'Tell me the name of the tumour.'

Rafiq is pacing up and down the length of the room and throws me glances I can't interpret.

'If you want to know,' my mother's voice comes through the receiver, 'although I'm not sure how that is supposed to make a difference because you are no doctor . . .' She pauses. 'It's a pituitary gland tumour.'

Pituitary gland, I repeat silently in order not to forget. Aloud I say, 'Mum, I will call you right back from my mobile.'

Rafiq stops pacing and sits down next to me on the sofa. He explains that the tumour is more than likely benign. The operation will be routine. On the other hand, no surgical intervention is without danger.

'Your mother is clearly frightened. You should go and see her.'

'But I want to stay here with you. Especially now.'

'*Habibi*, we can't do anything here. Go and see her.'

~

The following day I catch the train to my parents. I hold my mother's hand in the hospital. The operation went well. She says I look like a nun. Over my *abaya* I am now wearing a *jilbab*, a poncho-like hijab that covers my entire upper body down to the knees.

I say, 'My garments create a space for inner peace, when outside war rages everywhere in the world.'

My father says, 'This situation was forced upon us. But it won't take long, we are sorting it out.'

'It is none of our business to sort anything out. Who are

we to think we can sort things out?' I reply, and try not to raise my voice.

My father shrugs his shoulders. 'Lydia, you need to learn to discuss matters coolly and without getting emotionally involved.'

I bend over my mother in the hospital bed and kiss her on the forehead, and I kiss my father's cheek at the train station and board the train with the baby in my tummy.

And I haven't mentioned the baby to them. My parents will never know about any of my babies. They will never know that their daughter was capable of conceiving. But she can't hold them. They don't want to stay with me, in my tummy. This useless tummy that is no good for anything, certainly not for carrying babies. This tummy that still belongs to Lydia, will always belong to Lydia. And I can call myself Kauthar as much as I want, Kauthar the river of abundance. But it is only a name, nothing but a name, empty and desolate, and inside me nothing can grow.

I lose my second baby in the tenth week.

I felt guilty because of my first baby. Then I thought God had forgiven me because He gave me Rafiq so I could conceive new life in praise of Him in the union with my husband. When I lose my second baby I know that He is angry with me. I have strayed off the path, have become a hypocrite without even noticing the changes. I still believe in Him, still pray, still fast. But do I sincerely and honestly contemplate His Being, think about Him, live and breathe in order to submit to His Glory?

Or have I indeed got caught once again in the web of this glittering, blinding world? I try to appease Him with hurried prayers – the compulsory parts only – and colourful hijabs and hippy skirts. Do I think about Him every waking minute? Do I speak His name when I go to bed? When I get up? When I leave the house? When I enter our flat? When I go to the bathroom? When I leave the bathroom? Before I step on the Tube? Before I look in a mirror? I often forget. And I haven't even noticed. Only now does it become apparent to me. When did I last attend a meeting of sisters? It's been a while. My free time I spend either alone or with Rafiq. We visit his uncle once a week and I see Mrs Alim once every other week. She has taken me under her wing and shows me how to cook Arabic meals, and we watch Egyptian soap operas, which she loves and I find loud and silly, but watching them at least improves my Arabic. Otherwise, I spend hours perfecting my calligraphy skills. And at work I joke with my colleagues.

'You are so much more relaxed since you got married,' the bespectacled David told me a few months after my wedding. 'If you weren't wearing a hijab one couldn't tell you were a Muslim.'

Back then, I responded to his comment by smiling. In my mind he was young and naive. There was no point trying to explain my religion to him. But now his remark comes to haunt me. It rings in my ears again and again. And I realize I have strayed too far from Him. I stay in bed for days. After the miscarriage the doctor writes me a week's sick note. Rafiq strokes my head, makes me tea and brings it to my bedside. He also says that from a medical point of view there is no reason why it won't work out next time. We should trust in Allah, he says. And everything will come good. Then he has to leave – either to go to the hospital or to see his friends and follow together the unfolding of the war in Iraq and wait for the inevitable catastrophe. When he isn't working nights, he still comes home in the early hours of the morning and sleeps on the sofa. 'In order not to wake you up, *habibi*.' He brings me flowers and chocolate. And on the phone I tell my parents that I have caught a bad cold. The doctor gives me two further weeks' sick leave.

'As I see from your notes,' the doctor says, peeling her eyes from the screen in front of her and looking at me, 'you had an abortion a few years ago.' She simply throws the sentence at me. And it lands at my feet.

'My situation was very different back then,' I reply calmly, and pray silently to Allah that I may leave this room quickly. This woman does not understand anything.

'May I ask you a personal question?'

I shrug my shoulders with an air of deliberate indifference.

'Your husband is a Muslim too?'

'Yes.'

'From which country is he?'

'I don't think I need to reply to this question.'

'Does your husband put you under pressure?'

'What do you mean?'

For a moment she hesitates, then she says, 'I mean, does he blame you for the miscarriage and would he like you to become pregnant again as quickly as possible?'

'My husband is a Muslim, just like I am a Muslim. Being a Muslim does not imply stupidity or primitivism.'

'Please don't misunderstand me. I am only trying to exclude certain factors. And I can only do that by starting at the beginning. I don't know your husband, but if he comes from a traditional Islamic country it could be that you and he too are confronted by certain expectations which at the moment you can't fulfil.'

'What you are talking about has nothing to do with Islam but is a question of culture, and this is something to which my husband does not subscribe. My beliefs – and my husband's – give me as much time and space as I need. No one is putting me under pressure – sexually or psychologically.'

~

No. No one is putting me under pressure. But God has shown me a sign and, in His all-embracing mercy, He gives me time to understand the sign. Time and space. And so I lie in bed and only get up to wash and pray. It seems as if my body doesn't want to function any longer. Only my mind doesn't stop working. Loneliness begins to envelop me.

It takes me many days to understand why God has shrouded me in this loneliness. Until I remember that once before I lay like this. Not in a bed. On a kitchen floor, drunk. And what happened afterwards? Afterwards, the next day, God sent me Rabia and led me on to the straight path.

~

I have walked a fair distance along this path. I believe in Him, I follow His laws and rules. But I have slowed down. Sometimes I pause and am distracted by nice things, worldly things on the wayside. Like Little Red Riding Hood who skipped into the forest and forgot the time while picking flowers. Yet God has a plan for me. He knows that I am capable of reaching my goal and that's why He wants to help me to get back on track and encourages me to continue unfalteringly. He knows that His sign will hurt me, must hurt me, for me to see. And I see and rise from my bed, *Bismillahi wa ala barakat Allah*. In the name of Allah and with His blessing. His breath enters me and straightens me and I walk on tall, with a firm step. And I know that when I become tired He will help me and He will reward me. I keep my gaze fixed on the path.

~

I now cover myself with a black chador and niqab when I leave our flat. I hand in my resignation at the library, because the jokes and banter of my male colleagues are inappropriate for a Muslim woman but I don't know how to stop them without appearing rude and unfriendly. So I decide to avoid these comments altogether by no longer working outside my home. Rafiq agrees with my decision. He knows how difficult I find the relationship with my male colleagues and that I prefer my own company. I now spend many hours listening to the Quran on CD. I want to learn to copy the words perfectly. Because only if I speak the language of the revelation perfectly will I be able to understand the revelation completely. Arabic is the language of the holy revelation. It is the language of the desert, the language of the hot wind, the gleaming sun. There we are aware of our infinite loneliness, there we are deprived of the most essential thing – water. There we have nothing – except Allah. My love of God is rekindled once more in blazing flames and my gratefulness burns anew because He has given us His book, the Quran. I now understand that I want to live my life in the name of the book. I no longer belong to the world outside the book.

∼

Rafiq says he would like to go to Baghdad for a few months to work in a hospital. They need qualified doctors. His current fixed-term contract is coming to an end. We start planning. He wants to go for six months. Initially we decide that I will travel with him. But then he changes his mind and convinces me to stay behind. 'I couldn't do my job properly, Kauthar, if I thought you might be in danger.' And he adds, '*Insh'Allah*.

God willing, nothing will happen to me. Allah won't allow it that I don't come back.'

On our final night I lie in his arms, then the next morning I accompany him to the airport and wave as he goes through passport control, and I think that I will never see him again. What am I doing in this city alone? A city that increasingly perceives me as a foreigner, even an enemy.

I lock up our flat and move to Mrs Alim's, while Mr Alim goes to a friend's place for the time that I am there.

'I will look after you,' Mrs Alim says, and laughs.

I stay with her for four weeks. Then I persuade her that it would be good for Mr Alim to come back for a few days. In the meantime, I say I will go to see my parents. A white lie. In our flat I leave the curtains drawn, as if I'm not at home. Rafiq calls but the connection is cut after about a minute. I hear an explosion in the background.

I visit my parents. It's the first time with chador and niqab.

'You can't possibly show yourself like this on the street,' my mother says straight away. 'Maybe in London, but not here.'

I ask why she minds. After all, inside the house she sees me in trackies and T-shirt.

'You are not going out wearing that,' she repeats. 'People will think you've gone completely mad.'

I say nothing. My mother goes outside to work in the garden, turning over the earth. I stay indoors, while my father gets ready to go for a run.

Before he goes I ask, 'Do you still do the pull-ups?'

'Yes, but only twenty-five,' he replies. 'Do you want to come with me?'

'Do you mind if I wear my niqab and chador?' I ask in return.

'Can't you do without those cloaks for once?'

'No, that's not possible,' I reply. Then I explain that his request is the equivalent to me asking him not to go jogging for a week, only one short week. And we both burst out laughing, my father and I, and he goes jogging on his own.

'Maybe it's best if you stay,' he adds as a last comment before leaving the house. 'At least your mother won't get upset.'

∼

They don't understand. They have no idea. And perhaps I would have liked them to understand and perhaps at that moment I didn't want them to understand any longer. I head back to London and a few days later I catch a plane to Amman. I still have a valid visa for Jordan and Iraq which we had arranged when we planned to go out to Iraq together. Only in Amman do I tell Rafiq on the phone that I am on my way to him. That I am waiting for a flight to Baghdad, that it might take a few days.

'Go back to London,' he says. 'Please. Life is hell here. I'll be with you in four months.'

I say, 'I am your wife. I should be where you are. You can't just leave me behind on the other side of the world. To do what? To wait? For what? To be told of your death. What am I doing in London? In a city, a world, I no longer belong to? I belong to you. At your side. We are husband and wife in the name of Allah, we belong together.'

I am standing in a telephone booth, staring at the traffic-jammed square. Cars blow their horns, have stopped in the middle of the road, wedged sideways. Voices shout and swear. Men in the cars, women in hijab or chador four or five in the back; only occasionally one without her head covered rushes past. No one pays any attention to me in the telephone booth. Outwardly I finally fit into the picture. There is a crackling on the line. Dust is burning my eyes. Has Rafiq said anything or is he waiting for me to continue?

He says, 'OK, then come. You are my wife and I love you.' Then he adds, 'You remember I told you about my young cousin Fatimah? The one I was supposed to have married a few years ago? When I arrived here, her mother was dying and I promised her I'd marry Fatimah. I am the only male relative she has left. The others have all died or been killed. In order to protect her I had to marry her.'

I had to marry her. I had to marry her. The sentence repeats itself in my ears. My eyes are burning even more. Sweat trickles down my temples beneath the veil. The rules of the game, I suddenly think. I have left one world behind and entered another. And in this world a man has the right to marry four wives. Remember, Kauthar, you know the rules better than he does: *And if ye fear that ye will not deal fairly by the orphans, marry of the women, who seem good to you, two or three or four; and if ye fear that ye cannot do justice to so many then one only*, I recite in my head in Arabic.

'Can you do justice to both of us?' I ask my husband.

'Kauthar, please, do try to understand. It's about survival. She is my relative. My blood relative. I can't just turn a blind eye. We are family.'

'And I, Rafiq, agree and accept your decision. I only want to know, can you do justice to both of us? Because that is the law of God, for all of us, in all situations, at all times.'

'I love you, *habibi*,' he says.

I love you, *habibi*. I love you, *habibi*. The words swirl around in my head and get jumbled up. Love you, *habibi*, I. I you, *habibi*, love. *Habibi*, darling. *Hubb*. *Habibi*. *Hubb*. Love. And in my head I search the Quran and I become increasingly certain about something I've already suspected. It's a human construction, without sense, without meaning, useless. A human lie. There is no mention of *hubb* – love – between man and woman in the Quran. It says: *They are raiment for you and ye are raiment for them*. It says: *And He ordained between you respect and mercy. Lo, herein indeed are portents for folk who reflect*. And I do reflect. No one can blame me for not reflecting.

Are we splitting hairs again? Dissecting individual words? Getting hung up on individual letters?

Yes, indeed. That is precisely what we're doing. I tell the voices in my head to be quiet. I am searching for the truth. I am getting close to understanding. I am getting closer and closer to

Him. I follow Him, only Him and His Prophet. And you want to prevent me, as you have always prevented me? Call this splitting hairs, dissecting words. Say, No, that's not the way to do it! Have you ever bothered to reflect, to look things up? Yes, you. All of you. I am not Lydia. I am Kauthar. The river of abundance. The source of bounty. Bubbling, pouring forth, making sense.

Everything is clear now. Only for a brief moment does it cross my mind that if I was still living in the world of appearances, the pain would break my heart. My husband has taken a second wife. Instead, however, I feel no pain. I feel something totally different. I feel joy. And pure joy makes my heart explode. Finally I am free of the monkey bar, free of the world of appearances. My release is successful. I am in the air. Love, true, real love, exists only between God and mankind. Only God can say to man, I love you, *uhibbuk*. And man can say to God, *Uhibbuk*. Because only between God and man does such love exists. *He loves them and they love Him. Yuhibbuhum wa yuhibbunahu.*

And I understand. The moment Rafiq says, I love you, *habibi*. Poor Rafiq. You can't love me and I can't love you. It's not possible. We have been blinded. *The world is a magician greater than Harut and Marut and you should avoid it.* I don't ever again want to hear from you that you love me. Do you hear me? Never again. It's all lies and deception. A glitter word invented by the glitter-glamour world. And I had thought that you and I would have nothing to do with this world . . .

~

Rafiq talks. He starts talking in the taxi from the airport – in the first taxi – then we change once, twice, three times in order to dodge the warring parties who all call themselves Muslims. They are in fact hypocrites. Allah and His Prophet warned them: *And hold fast, all of you together, to the rope of Allah, and do not become divided.* But they have become divided and they fight each other.

And Rafiq says, 'It is a temporary marriage for Fatimah's protection. So I can protect her and her four-year-old son, Hassan. Without male protection they'd be lost. Her husband was a victim of Saddam's regime. I am looking for another husband for her. I have not touched her.'

'Why haven't you touched her? She is your wife. Don't you desire her?'

'I don't want to touch her. You are my wife. I want to touch you.'

'If you touch me, you have to touch her. That's what the law says. She has become your wife in the name of Allah. You are no longer just my husband. You belong to her too.'

'You are talking nonsense.'

'I support your decision to marry a second woman. According to the law, you should have asked me, your first wife, but you didn't. You have sinned before God. Only God can forgive you. But I can help you not be a hypocrite. Because I don't want to be married to a hypocrite. And anyway, she will be able to give you what I am not capable of providing: children.'

Rafiq takes my hand, which is resting between us on the seat.

'Kauthar, please don't talk like this. We will have children together, you and I. When my contract has finished, we'll go back home, to London. I had to come here. But I now understand that I can't live here. I am ashamed and I ask Allah and my father for forgiveness every single day. To forgive me for being so weak. I didn't want you to come. I wanted to survive these months, sort out the situation with Fatimah and get back to you.'

Later he is crying like a baby and I take him in my arms. We are sharing the bed of his dead aunt. Next door Fatimah and Hassan are sleeping on the couch. I rock Rafiq back and forth and stroke his head gently.

'I feel so stupid. Like a little boy who is suddenly forced to face the real world. Ever since we arrived with my mother in London my dream has always been to return "home" – home to my country. I'd be free of the guilt I felt because of my father. I'd finally live in an Islamic country. London was an intermediate stop, a temporary solution out of necessity. And suddenly I realize that all this time I have been chasing a childish dream, while at the same time happiness was staring me right in the face. Kauthar, people in London – and by that I mean Christians, Jews, Shiites, Sunnis, Hindus, atheists, everyone, whatever their colour and whatever their religion –

live more together in the name of Allah, in the name of peace, than here. I wish it wasn't true. I wish I had the conviction that I should stay here and fight for the Islamic *ummah*. I have asked Allah for it, I have prayed for it. But I don't have that conviction. I am scared, Kauthar.'

And he is crying again, and he holds on to me tight and buries his face in the side of my neck.

'Hold me.'

And I hold him in my arms and rock him back and forth and I open myself to him and become one with him, Rafiq, my husband.

~

When he has fallen asleep, I get up and wake Fatimah and tell her to lie next to him in the bed. At first she doesn't understand. My foreign accent sounds strange to her. I explain that she has a duty towards her husband. I have shared the first half of the night with him, now she has to share the second half with him. She shakes her head and pulls the blanket up to her chin. I bend down towards her and hiss into her ear that if she refuses to fulfil her marital duties towards her husband, I'll convince Rafiq in the morning to divorce her. So she gets up and walks into the next room and closes the door behind her. I lie down besides Hassan on the couch and move as close as possible to his little body without waking him. I breathe in the warm smell of his hair. I close my eyes and hear shellfire in the distance. I put my arm around Hassan and hope he doesn't wake up, because then he'd cry and call for his mother.

When dawn breaks I get up and fill the round plastic bowl with water and take it to the toilet, a tiny square room with a hole in the ground. I wet my body from head to toe, then I wash my hands with soap and clean my mouth and my nose. I perform *ghusl janabat*, the full-body ablution. *Qurbatan illa Allah*, to be close to God. Once again I pour water over my hair. Then I shampoo it. I rub soap into my neck, my right shoulder, my right arm, my right breast, the right half of my bottom, the right leg, the right foot. Then the left side. As I straighten up, a light breeze touches me. I look up to the small open window. A bird flies past. And I notice the absence of shellfire. It is quiet. Many years ago, when I was another person who was called Lydia, she too used to get up early, at five, four thirty, sometimes four o'clock. It was always quiet during those early-morning hours. She would sit at her desk and study. Everyone else was asleep, so there was no danger of being disturbed. She would feel calm and able to concentrate on her work, confident in the knowledge that everything that should have happened happened yesterday and everything that should happen will happen with the new day. But the new day hasn't yet arrived and Kauthar is standing in the little room, legs apart above the earth closet, the smell of cheap soap on her body, a lovely fresh breeze on her face. And there are no bombs falling and no shellfire and the muezzin hasn't yet called out for the morning prayer and Rafiq, her husband, and Fatimah, his second wife, and Hassan, her young son, are asleep. Kauthar sees Lydia at her desk, bent over her homework, and for a fleeting moment her heart aches for Lydia, for the girl she once was, who she never wanted to be, who she shouldn't have been. And if Kauthar were able to cry, she would. She bends forward, takes the bowl and pours the rest of the water over her head.

Hassan is still asleep on the couch. No one seems to stir in the other room. I knock on the door to wake them for prayer. 'Rafiq! Fatimah!' I call out quietly. I am turning away from the door when suddenly it swings wide open.

'Have you gone completely mad!' Rafiq's voice thunders out into the front room.

At the same moment shellfire starts somewhere. Hassan jolts upright and bursts into tears. I spin round towards Rafiq, who is standing in the door between the two rooms. Behind him I spot Fatimah, who is getting up from a prayer mat she has slept on. Rafiq and I are staring at each other. Fatimah pushes past our husband, rushes towards her son, pulls him into her arms. She is wearing the dress in which she slept all night. Rafiq has wrapped the blanket around his waist and is holding it tight with one hand.

'It's time for prayer,' I say calmly. 'You should get ready.'

'Kauthar!' Rafiq shouts with such force that spit sprays out of his mouth.

Hassan sobs convulsively, lifts his hands and presses them

against his ears. Fatimah talks to him quietly. I throw a quick glance at mother and child. Then I turn back to Rafiq.

'You should not lose control in front of your son,' I say.

'Get into the room,' Rafiq commands.

I don't move. Hassan's sobs are suddenly overpowered by a loud clicking sound. The muezzin from the mosque on the other side of the road has turned on his microphone. He coughs, clears his throat.

A-lla-hu-ak-bar! Allah is the Greatest!

'You can't pray like this,' I say to Rafiq. 'You need to wash. You slept with your wives last night.'

Rafiq stumbles forward two steps, grabs my arm, pulls me into the bedroom and shuts the door with a bang. We stand facing each other. He is still holding the blanket with one hand around his waist.

'Have you lost your senses?'

A-lla-hu-ak-bar!

I shake my head. My upper arm, where Rafiq grabbed me, is burning. Muhammad, peace be upon Him, ordered men not to physically abuse their wives. But I don't say this out loud.

'I am a Muslim. I live according to the sharia, the Islamic law,' I say slowly and deliberately. I feel it's important for Rafiq to understand what I say. Because only if he understands will it be possible for me to continue being his wife.

A-lla-hu-ak-bar!

'As a Muslim woman I am allowed to marry only a Muslim man,' I continue.

A-lla-hu-ak-bar!

'My husband, you have now executed your right to take a second wife. I support your decision because it is Allah's law. I see it as an opportunity yet again to show God my deep trust in Him.'

The muezzin lowers his voice. *Ashadu alla ilaha illallah* – I testify that there is no god except Allah.

'I have to help you to stay on the right path, Rafiq. Did you let Fatimah sleep on the cold floor last night? She belongs in bed with you. Don't just choose the rules that suit you. You can't do that. Allah will see through you.'

Ashadu alla ilaha illallah. No God except Allah.

'I will have to file for divorce if I realize that you are no longer a true Muslim.'

~

While I speak Rafiq doesn't take his eyes off me. Disbelief. Naked disbelief is written all over his face. Where is the Rafiq I know, whom I married, with whom I became one in the name of Allah? Instead I am staring at a doubting man. I lift my arm. I want to shake him, wake him up, free him from the devil's embrace in which he is lost. But I lower my arm.

'Rafiq, come back to God, please. I beg you,' I whisper, and fall to my knees in front of him and fling my arms around his legs. 'Don't leave me. Don't leave your religion. I will help you.'

Rafiq crouches down, then sits with his back against the wall on the floor and pulls me towards him. He strokes my hair.

'Kauthar, I love you. I don't want to sleep with Fatimah. You are my wife. My only wife. And Allah is my witness. I should not have left you behind in London on your own. You are suffering from depression. As a doctor, I can see this now. You and I need to go back as quickly as possible, so you can receive treatment.'

I straighten up, free myself from him, move away.

And now I do start to cry after all, now Kauthar begins to cry for Rafiq, who no longer is her Rafiq, for her marriage, which no longer is a marriage, which no longer can be a marriage. Because Rafiq has gone astray.

'You have lost your faith. May God forgive you, Rafiq.'

For a moment Rafiq doesn't move. Then he says, 'I will find a new husband for Fatimah and get us both back to London on the next possible flight.'

He stands up, fetches his clothes, which are lying on the only chair in the room, and dresses with his back against the door. At the same time I pick up the mat on which Fatimah slept last night and turn it towards Ka'abah. I look around the bare room for something to cover my hair.

'I have to pray,' I say to Rafiq, who is buckling his belt. 'I need a hijab.'

He opens the door and asks Fatimah to hand him my chador. She gives it to him without saying a word and he passes it to me. I pull the garment over my head and while I am standing upright with my hands by my side, ready to commence my prayer, Rafiq leaves the room. My prayer stone is in my bag next door but I don't want to go there and I know Allah will forgive me.

I sink into prayer. Each single word enters my body, my heart, as if never heard before but at the same time as ancient as mankind, so utterly familiar.

~

I cower against the wall opposite the door. Again and again I strain to hear if Rafiq has come back. I am waiting and hoping and praying to God that He may guide my husband. I am willing to forgive him, but forgiveness is not mine to give. Only God can forgive. I arrange the chador around my body and pull the veil over my face so that there is only a little opening for my eyes.

~

When the door opens and Fatimah indicates I should follow her, I am not in the least surprised.

She whispers, 'There are men in the other room. The brother of my first husband and his friends.'

I stand up and rearrange my chador and make sure that my hairline is covered. I adjust the niqab. I step into the next room. A big lake of thick blood covers the floor. A man is lying in the middle of it.

'An American soldier shot him,' I hear Fatimah say. 'If we move him, he will die. You have to run to the hospital and fetch Rafiq.'

I stare at the red puddle, thick as oil paint. Thick red. Everywhere blood.

'Kauthar! You have to get Rafiq. Quickly. Here is your passport. They've blocked the roads downstairs. But you with your British passport will get past the soldiers.'

'Where is the hospital?' I ask.

Fatimah explains it to me. I can't miss it. I am about to ask, Why is this man here? Why have they shot him? But Fatimah pushes me out of the door.

'Quick. Hurry. He is bleeding to death. Can't you see?'

I run down the stairs. The lift, if it ever worked, has obviously not been in use for ages. As I step outside, the hot, dusty dry air takes my breath away. I look to the right, down the narrow unpaved road. A few blocks away a tank is parked right across the road. Soldiers with helmets and machine guns are standing in front of it. I can spot no other living soul, but I can sense them behind the walls of the houses, behind the windows, and as I start walking towards the tank and the soldiers I feel their invisible eyes on me.

'Stop. No further!' American accent.

What if I didn't speak or even understand English? A gloved hand with fingers spread wide on an outstretched arm indicates that I can go no further. I stop and hold out my passport.

'I am British,' I say. 'I have to get to the hospital at the end of the road.'

The soldier, a boy really, surely no older than twenty, takes my passport, flicks through it. He is ready for combat in his camouflage battledress, helmet, ammunition belt, knee- and elbow-protectors. Dark sunglasses cover his eyes; only his nose, mouth and part of his cheeks are visible. Still, a name tag on his jacket tells me he is 'Johnson'. I wonder what colour his eyes are.

'Remove the veil,' Johnson commands.

I lift my veil.

'Remove it completely,' he barks.

I shake my head, let the niqab drop down over my face again.

'No,' I say. 'Even at passport control in London it's enough to raise it. You've seen my face.'

'We are not British passport control here. We are in Baghdad. Remove your veil. We won't discuss it. If you want to pass this control, you have to remove your veil.'

I am thinking about the man up on the eighth floor in the pool of blood. It might have even been this soldier who shot him. Playing his war games, giving himself airs, as if he has a right to be here, as if there is anyone here wanting to play with him. But this is no playground and Lydia is no longer hanging from the monkey bar upside-down, scared of letting go.

I remove the niqab.

'OK. Now legs apart, arms wide.'

I look up into the blue sky while Johnson runs the gun barrel across my body.

'Where are you staying?'

I point to the block of flats.

The soldier hands me back my passport and points alongside the tank.

'You can go.'

I fasten my niqab and continue along the ghost road. I can hear noise from parallel streets, but here nothing moves. I pass a burnt-out car. The windows in the house behind it are shattered. Shreds of curtain blow in the wind. I turn round, look back to the tank. From this side, too, soldiers are guarding the checkpoint, machine guns at the ready.

~

Noisy chaos meets me at the hospital. Human bodies are sitting, standing, laying, sleeping, arguing, praying, eating. Sick and wounded and dead. In between men – and a few women – in white coats dart about like lost white dots. I approach one of them, ask for Rafiq. He points down a corridor. I ask another one and then another one. I finally see him, huddled on a chair, a cup of water in his hand. He looks tired and thin. I hadn't noticed up until now.

'Rafiq!' I kneel down next to him, place my hand on his knee.

'Kauthar!' He looks up in surprise. 'What are you doing

here?' He sounds immensely tired. All the anger from this morning has evaporated. Has he forgotten?

'Fatimah sent me. You have to come. They brought someone with a bullet wound. We don't have much time. He is bleeding to death in the flat.'

'Do you know who he is?'

He has placed his hand above mine on his knee. I see his greasy hair, the dark circles under his eyes. I would love to take him in my arms, like a mother holding her son. I find it difficult to keep in my mind what happened between us this morning.

~

And if we stay here and don't move, would everything that has happened not have happened? And after an eternity would we get up and return to London, to walk once again hand in hand on the Heath?

~

But I am already saying the next words: 'I think it's the brother of Fatimah's first husband.'

Rafiq shakes his head. 'Ahmed, that fool. It was predictable.'

'What?' I ask.

'I'll explain later. Not now.'

He puts the cup on the floor. 'Wait here. I'll be back in a second. I just have to let a colleague know that I am going.'

~

We are running back along detours to avoid the checkpoint. Since we are running, we can't talk. We approach the building from the other side and enter through the cellar. And only when we are in front of the flat does Rafiq turn around to me.

'Kauthar, whatever is spoken about in there, you have to trust me, I have nothing to do with it.'

'I don't understand,' I say.

'All I know is that Ahmed, Fatimah's brother-in-law, hangs out with Muqtada al-Sadr's Mahdi Army. Officially they provide security against looters, but lately they have also launched attacks.'

Inside Fatimah is sitting cross-legged on the floor, holding the head of the wounded man. A young man with a beard is sitting against the wall. The others have gone. Rafiq rips open the blood-drenched shirt of the injured man. A gaping chest wound like the mouth of a fish out of water appears. Bile travels up my throat and into my mouth.

'Cut his trousers. I need to see his leg.'

The young man with the beard rushes to the kitchen. I swallow the bile. He returns with a knife. In the meantime Rafiq has pulled a pack of medical equipment out from underneath his shirt. He grabs a morphine ampoule and injects it into the leg that isn't bleeding.

They shift the wounded man on to one side. Rafiq's motionless face does not reveal what he sees at the back. They roll the body to its initial position. Rafiq applies gauze pads to the chest wound, then inserts a tube. The man starts coughing. Blood bubbles up out of his mouth. Fatimah bends further over his head, trying to soothe him. For a moment the image freezes. Suddenly I hear Fatimah's wailing. And Rafiq pulls the tube out and throws it on to the floor, jumps up, walks to the wall and smashes his fist against it.

'That idiot!' he shouts.

I take a step towards him. He turns around.

'Don't.'

He raises his hands and shakes his head at me. I hesitate but something in his face tells me not to approach. I step back towards the wall. Rafiq closes his eyes and breathes deeply.

'Why?' he asks as he opens his eyes again.

'Because we have to do something,' the man replies, staring at Rafiq.

'Like getting yourselves killed? How is that going to help?' Rafiq starts pacing the room.

'We are fighting against al-Dajjal, the Deceiver, who has invaded our country. This is our chance to ensure that a just Shia caliphate will be established in our country.'

'To establish a just Shia caliphate?'

'If we don't fight now we will lose everything to the invaders and Sunni traitors. We owe it to our people to fight. We owe it to Allah. It is our duty to strive towards an Islamic *ummah* here on earth. We will be rewarded in Paradise.'

'Rewarded? In Paradise? For blowing up Americans?'

'Listen to you, brother! Shame on you. Remember your father. Remember all the Shiites who betrayed Allah by hiding their belief. Who refused to obey Allah's command. No one can help the ones who have turned their backs on Allah.'

For a few moments Rafiq and the young man stare at each other silently. Then Rafiq slowly lifts both his arms and removes the other's hands from his shoulders. He steps aside and turns towards Fatimah, who has now started to hit her face with her blood-stained hands, rocking back and forth, her face contorted into a soundless scream of pain. I see Rafiq walking towards her and helping her to her feet. He is leading her to one of the big cushions lying on the floor against the wall. She sits down and he kneels next to her. He wipes the hair out of her face and then, with a piece of cloth, wipes the blood from her face and hands. I suddenly remember Hassan. I find him crouching behind the door and want to pick him up. But he moves away from me, jumps up and runs to his mother. The other young men reappear and take the corpse away. I am standing pressed against the wall; no one takes any notice of me. Fatimah and her son lie down on the bed next door. And only when Rafiq has gone back to the hospital do I realize that my body is still able to move in this world.

～

I scrub the floor.

Afterwards I go to the kitchen and search for something

131

to eat for Fatimah, Hassan and myself. I find two eggs in the fridge and a few tomatoes and an onion in a basket. I open the cupboards looking for a frying pan and when I open the door underneath the sink there is the ammunition belt. Or at least at first glance I think it is an ammunition belt, because it looks just like the toy ammunition belt my brother used to own as a boy. Only three times wider. I hesitate, staring at it, and think about closing the door again and pretending I've not seen it. But it's lying on the pan. I have to lift it if I want the frying pan. Carefully, I pick it up. I am scared it will explode. Then I see the blood. It is the belt with the explosives that Fatimah's brother-in-law wore. She must have hidden it here. Or did she? Did she know, did He know, that I would pass by here on my way to Him? I did not search for the belt or the explosives. I came across them on my path.

I take the pan and return the belt to its place. I cook an omelette and wake Fatimah. She sits up and shakes her head at the plate. She doesn't want to eat. I bring the plate closer to her nose.

'Eat! Otherwise your next husband won't like you.'

She takes the plate, leans back against the headrest of the bed, pulls her legs up and obediently lifts a fork to her mouth. Hassan is still asleep. I sit down on the bed.

'The belt,' I say. 'I found the belt.'

She shakes her head without looking me in the eyes.

'What will happen to the belt?'

She doesn't answer. Instead she moves away from me,

closer to her son. She is scared of me. She was scared of me from the beginning. Like all of them are scared of me.

'I'm asking you what will happen to the belt?'

She shrugs her shoulders, mumbles, 'I don't know.'

'Does Rafiq know?'

'No, no.' For the first time she is looking me straight in the eyes. Frightened. 'Please, don't say anything.'

'I won't tell him. But in exchange you must tell me what you are going to do with the belt. Will the guys who were here this morning fetch it later?'

'I don't know. I honestly don't know.'

She is crying now. 'Rafiq is such a good man. He shouldn't know.'

'Eat,' I order, and with a movement of my head I point to the plate. 'He won't ever know.'

Then I get up, leave the room and pull the door shut behind me.

I wash myself and say the afternoon prayer. All birth-giving is painful. Nothing new is born without pain. Once upon a time Paradise was situated between the Tigris and the Euphrates; today war rages here. But what does this war symbolize if not birth pangs, so that once again a Garden of Eden will flourish and grow? War rages, but this war is not terrible. It can't be terrible, because Allah willed it since it exists. Only that which Allah wills exists. In reality, in the true reality that is Allah's reality, this war is an expression of the desire for true life, which can only be a yearning towards Him, towards His Paradise.

I grasp this knowledge and I cup my hands and extend my arms towards Him. And I offer myself to Him gratefully, with devotion and with humility.

~

In the days that follow I refuse any intimate relationship with Rafiq, even though I know it could be considered a sin. But as far as I am concerned he is no longer my husband.

I tell him I want a divorce.

He replies, 'Kauthar, *habibi*, in ten days we will fly back to Amman and then hopefully as soon as possible on to London. Everything will be all right.'

He tries to put his arm round me, but I don't want to be touched by him.

~

'Snap!'

Rafiq and Hassan sit on the floor. Rafiq brought the cards back from the hospital.

'Snap!'

Hassan falls back, laughing. Rafiq sits cross-legged. He smiles and waits patiently until Hassan has straightened up again.

'Ready?' He looks at the boy with a wicked sparkle in his eye.

Hassan gleams back at him, giggling in anticipation. He nods. Holds his breath. Then screams 'Ready!' and throws his card down and straight away his hand on top. 'Snap! Snap! Snap!'

Rafiq points his finger at the boy. 'Show me!'

Hassan shakes his head.

'I will tickle you.' Rafiq laughs.

'Tickle me! Tickle me!' screams the boy.

And Rafiq leaps forward, grabs the boy and pulls him on to his lap, tickling him while making roaring noises. 'I will tickle you and eat you alive.'

I turn my head and see Fatimah standing in the doorway to the bedroom. She stares at Rafiq and the boy, motionless. Suddenly the giggling and roaring stop. I turn my head back to Rafiq and Hassan. The boy now lies in Rafiq's arm like a baby. He has put a hand on Rafiq's cheek.

'Can we come with you to London?' he then asks.

For a moment I feel the silence as thick as mud around us. Rafiq looks at the boy in his arms.

'You can't. I am so sorry.' Rafiq strokes Hassan's head.

'Hassan!' Fatimah calls, and has stepped inside the room. She takes hold of her son's free arm and pulls him out of Rafiq's lap. 'You need to sleep.' She tries to drag the boy with her towards the bedroom, but Hassan tears himself away and flies back into Rafiq's lap.

'I want to play snap,' he cries, and presses his face against Rafiq's cheek.

Rafiq puts his arm around Hassan and for a moment holds the boy tight. Then he lifts him up and sets him on his feet in front of him.

'Hassan, you are a big boy. You need to go to sleep now and tomorrow you will move in with Uncle Haydar.'

The boy starts shaking his head wildly from side to side.

'I don't want to. I don't want to. I want to stay with you.'

Before Rafiq can say anything else, Fatimah lifts her son off his feet and carries him, screaming and kicking, into the bedroom.

~

Rafiq talks about our children, the house we will eventually own with a little back garden. And I think, How about a car, two cars, one garage, two garages, three garages? One for table tennis. And perhaps our children might receive some medals, too? As I once did.

~

I open my eyes and my gaze falls on a beautiful little box on my bedside table. It's dark blue with white stars and a silver ribbon. I pull my hand from underneath the blanket and touch the box with my fingertips. I had so hoped that my father would bring me a present. It was my birthday yesterday. I am seven years old now. My father missed my birthday because he was away on an assignment. He returned late last night.

'Why don't you open it?'

My father sits down on the end of my bed. For a moment I lie still. Then I sit up, take the little box and shift back on the bed so that I can lean against the wall. My father moves to sit next to me.

'Open it,' he encourages me. 'I can't wait to see what's inside.'

'You know what's inside,' I reply. 'It's from you.'

'Well,' he says with a smile, 'you need to open it to see if it's from me.'

I push the bow back, lift the lid. Whatever is inside is covered with a yellow cotton pad. I don't remove it immediately. As I bend over it, I feel my father's head very close; his chin touches my temple. I feel his breath. Together we are staring at the cotton pad, waiting to see what is underneath it. Then I take it between the thumb and middle finger of my right hand. We lower our heads even closer to the box. My face is now leaning against my father's cheek.

Lydia has never been this close to her father before. She usually worries that he doesn't like it when she sits on his lap. She presses her forehead against his forehead. She adapts her breathing to his. She hasn't yet lifted the little yellow pad, although she is holding it between her fingers. She feels her father's breathing, the beating of his temple. She doesn't move. And she no longer feels the little pad between her fingers. And she is no longer interested in what's in the box. All that counts right now is that her father isn't moving. She knows that he, too, wants to stay like this, to feel her close, to feel her breath, her face next to his. And she opens her fingers and the cotton pad falls to the bed. The little box slips out of her hands. She gets up on to her knees and raises her arms and turns towards her father. He still doesn't move. His head is now at the height of her face. And she throws both arms around his neck. His face turns towards her and she presses her body against his. Her fingers dig into his shaven neck and she closes her eyes and she kisses him on the lips. And she feels his lips and his stubble itch, and from television she knows that true lovers when they kiss turn their heads right to left and left to right while they continue pressing their lips tightly together. And so she turns her head a little bit to the right and a little bit to the left, without taking her lips from her father's lips. She stops kissing him and removes her lips from his and opens her eyes and looks into his face, so close, so big, so beautiful.

'I love you,' she whispers. 'I know the present is from you.'

She wants to press herself against him once more. Very firmly, very tight. For ever.

But then she hears her mother's voice. 'What's going on here?' Her mother is standing in the doorway.

'Look!' Her father picks up the little jewellery box and pulls out a necklace. It's a beautiful, thick purple ribbon with a silver medal at the end. Her father's silver medal, his very first medal, which he won when he was only a few years older than Lydia during the Commonwealth Youth Championships.

But her mother is angry: 'You can't give your medal to a seven-year-old girl! She'll lose it.'

And the mother takes the medal and locks it away in a drawer inside her wardrobe.

～

When Fatimah leaves I wonder if she's taken the belt. But it is still in the cupboard underneath the sink.

～

And Rafiq says, 'In five days, *habibi*, we will leave.'

But Kauthar senses that here in Baghdad she has come much closer to the truth than ever before. Allah makes it easy for her, for me. Still, to walk this path requires courage and strength in order to distinguish between the world of appearances and deception and the real world. In the world of appearances everyone believes that our individual lives matter and that death is a loss. The world of appearances deceives us. And so it is impossible to see that we are part of something much bigger. That we are part of God's world, of God's life. Only God's infinite life exists and for us He created Paradise. The life of the individual doesn't count, doesn't actually exist. It's an illusion. And therefore nothing is lost when the illusion disappears.

～

I pass the checkpoint. I am waved through now. The infidels who hide their blind eyes behind sunglasses wave me through with a nod, with a smile of recognition on their lips. They no longer ask for my passport. They know me now. But not everyone who passes the checkpoint is waved through. Neither the old woman who lives in the flat beneath us nor Rafiq, who has given up trying to circumnavigate the checkpoint. They search him each time.

And I pass the soldiers' checkpoint with a smile on my lips and a nod of the head.

~

In the hospital I look for Rafiq. I see him bending over a stretcher that rests on the floor among a group of wailing women. I push through the group and stand straight opposite Rafiq on the other side. A man lies on the stretcher. Hundreds of little cuts have disfigured his face. Rafiq is preparing an injection.

'Rafiq,' I say.

He puts the needle in the man's arm.

I don't know what I want here. I don't know what I want from Rafiq. Or rather, I didn't know a moment ago. Now I know.

'Rafiq,' I repeat.

I want him to answer, so that I can be sure that I actually said his name and that I can then reach out and touch him. Just briefly, a fleeting touch. He gestures towards the two men who stand at either end of the stretcher to lift it. They make their way through the crowd down the corridor. Rafiq is holding the drip. He didn't hear or see me.

~

I have gone too far ahead on the path to Allah. Rafiq is no longer able to see me. He became tired. Deviated from the path. He is lost. He needs to find his way again. Then he will follow me, I am sure. I will wait for him in Allah's Paradise. Rafiq has to complete the journey on his own and then we will be together again. Then he will be worthy of me once more and can once more be my husband in the name of God. I will give hope by setting an example, by providing a sign, a light that will shine through the fog and show the path more clearly for the ones who are following me. And even if they are blind they will still be able to feel the heat from the light on their cheeks.

I leave the hospital. Two teenage boys step on to the road a few metres in front of me from a side entrance to the hospital. They are pushing a wooden cart piled high with boxes. Skinny, scarred legs stick out of cropped Adidas trackies. Plastic sandals are kicking up dust. The wheels squeak. They are heading straight for the checkpoint. The top box wobbles dangerously for a second or two. Then it falls. A scream escapes one of the boys. They stop the cart, jump forward to collect the spilt contents. Syringes. A hundred or more. I walk past the boys. The syringes have already nearly all disappeared back into the box. I look towards the soldiers. They see what I have seen. I hear the wheels behind me move. I hold out my passport. Johnson waves me through. I continue on my way. I expect the squeaking of the wheels to stop. It doesn't. I turn my head, glancing over my shoulder. The boys follow close behind me. The soldiers are looking in the opposite direction. I keep on walking, go past the tank. Suddenly the squeaking turns off to the left. Once more I look over my shoulder and I see the boys with their spoils disappear into a house. The soldiers on this side appear like motionless wax figures.

Once upon a time I ran the risk of misunderstanding, of interpreting cunning enemy plots for genuine friendliness. But now I won't be deceived. I can see through their game. The game of life. Nothing but a game.

∾

I am looking out of the window. I can see them way down below me. The enemy soldiers. And I see them stopping a group of small schoolchildren with their teacher. Machine guns at the ready. I could help them and free them from their false world, from their world of deception. I could help my brothers and sisters to build a paradise here in this world, if only I am courageous enough to try the bar dismount without assistance one more time. Like I did when I was a girl hanging from the monkey bar in the playground. There I practised for the first time. And God gave me a sign. For a moment He took me into His reality. But He, the All-Knowing, knew what I was ignorant of. That I would improve. He will be proud of me.

∾

I pull the door shut behind me. I carefully put one foot in front of the other as I walk down the stairs. What if the explosives don't work and they shoot me? If it is His intention that I give a sign, I will give a sign. I walk upright, the control of my body comes from the core, from the depths of my stomach. I open the main door and step outside into the shadow of the apartment block. A skinny grey cat darts across the road and disappears down an alley. Two fat rats follow. I step forward. I am wearing my dark-blue shiny gymnast's outfit. Tightly fitted like a swimsuit. Sequins adorn my neckline. My back is straight and I lift my arm to indicate to the jury that I am ready. My ponytail is bobbing up and down as I walk towards the asymmetric bars. I adjust the hand-guards. Rub the chalk in. I walk along the unpaved dusty road. At the edges on both sides flat bungalows sit next to high-rise flats. It is quiet, very quiet. And it reeks. The rubbish hasn't been collected since the checkpoint was set up. It has piled up in front of the buildings. The audience holds its breath, waiting in anticipation. The narrow street in front of me lies in the shade. But I can see the light at the other end even though the tank is blocking the way. Two soldiers are staring right at me, like everyone else

– the audience, the cameras, the world. There will be photos and the film of my routine will be repeated on the news worldwide. I now notice another soldier, who is leaning out of the hatch at the top, his left arm hanging casually over the edge. I raise my arm to indicate that I am ready to begin my routine. And in that very moment the soldier's watch catches the sun. And I know it's His sign. My belly knows what to do. I swing. I hear shouts, shouts from the audience. They are applauding. I spread my legs and bring my hips into a deep body fold. The Endo circle. A beautiful feeling takes hold of my body. I am flying weightlessly, effortlessly. The routine is going well. My feet initiate the turn and the bar is released. I am now in the full-flight phase. Then I grasp again one more time.

I pull the lever.

My body is fully extended. I am airborne.

And I know that this time I will land with confidence on both feet, knees slightly bent.

ALSO BY MEIKE ZIERVOGEL

Magda (978-1-907773-40-2)
Clara's Daughter (978-1-907773-79-2)

NEW FICTION FROM SALT

KERRY HADLEY-PRYCE
The Black Country (978-1-78463-034-8)

IAN PARKINSON
The Beginning of the End (978-1-78463-026-3)

CHRISTOPHER PRENDERGAST
Septembers (978-1-907773-78-5)

JONATHAN TAYLOR
Melissa (978-1-78463-035-5)

GUY WARE
The Fat of Fed Beasts (978-1-78463-024-9)

ALSO AVAILABLE FROM SALT

ELIZABETH BAINES

Too Many Magpies (978-1-84471-721-7)

The Birth Machine (978-1-907773-02-0)

LESLEY GLAISTER

Little Egypt (978-1-907773-72-3)

ALISON MOORE

The Lighthouse (978-1-907773-17-4)

The Pre-War House and Other Stories (978-1-907773-50-1)

He Wants (978-1-907773-81-5)

ALICE THOMPSON

Justine (978-1-78463-031-7)

The Falconer (978-1-78463-009-6)

The Existential Detective (978-1-78463-011-9)

Burnt Island (978-1-907773-48-8)